How He Made Me Feel

Kendra Filch

Contents

Chapter 1 New Friends?

Chapter 1 New Friends

"Great. just my luck, stupid car," I said as my car suddenly stopped.

I'm going to be late. I can't be late.

Of course, this would happen to me today, out of all days.

It's not every day that a journalist like me would have the chance to do a one-on-one interview with a football player.

Well, not just a regular football player. A good one at that. One that everyone has been dying to get the chance to interview.

Jesse Hutcherman is the top football player for the Packers.

"Ugh, what the hell? I'm just going to get an Uber." I said, taking out my phone and requesting an Uber driver on the app.

Thank God I left early, or I would have been late.

I waited outside my building for the Uber driver; I got in the driver's car when he pulled up in front of my building. As soon as I got in, I told him I would give him a nice tip if he stepped on it.

He stepped on it, and in less than fifteen minutes, I saw myself in front of my destination. I gave him a thirty-dollar tip.

I didn't miss the Uber driver's expression of appreciation as he thanked me and helped me with my items.

After getting all my things from the Uber driver, I thanked him and said goodbye.

I turned to look at the hotel in front of me.

I took a few breaths, trying to give myself a pep talk, before I walked into the hotel building.

I headed towards the reception desk. My interview with the client, Jesse, was at the Hotel of Janboin Botanique. I smiled at her.

"Hi, I'm Ben Armstrong. I'm here to interview Jesse Hutcherman, I should be on the list of people allowed in the room. Can you please tell me where his room is?" I said to the lady.

She smiled at me and said, "Sure hun but let me give the room a call just to make sure that he is inspecting you right now, okay?"

I nodded my head. "Yes that's fine." I said.

I understand why she had to check; it's better to be safe after all, especially with all the crazy things happening.

"You may go to room 207, have a lovely day Mr. Armstrong." She said.

"Thank you, you as well Ma'am." I said, nodding my head to her as I turned to walk towards the elevator.

"What a nice looking young man." I heard her say as I walked away.

Entering the elevator, I decided to look at my reflection, wondering what the woman had seen.

I didn't think I was nice-looking. I've heard people say this about me before, among other things, but it was something that I never noticed myself or gave too much attention to. I looked at my reflection; I had blue eyes and reddish-blonde hair.

I've heard people mention that I should do modeling instead of journalism. But being a journalist fits me well. I didn't have a specific category I would stick to; I liked covering any category and story.

I walked out of the elevator and headed towards the room. "Room 204, 205, 206, 207 there we go room 207." I knocked three times on the door. I heard someone yell out, "Come in!"

A deep voice. For some reason, I found myself not able to move.

It was a pleasant voice, and I had no idea why I was still standing in front of the hotel door, thinking about this man's voice.

What the hell, why do I feel like this? I shook the feeling away and headed in.

"Mr. Hutcherman?" I said, looking for him, but I couldn't find him. I put my equipment and notebook on the coffee table.

"Hey, sorry man just got out the shower. You're early." I looked up, stunned. Not knowing what to say, one thing I was not expecting was this man to come out of the shower with just a towel on. Another thing is this man was attractive. He had tattoos all over his body, and he had good-looking ones, too. His hair was wet and pulled back. I stared away from him, not knowing how long I was staring at him.

I've never seen a picture of him; I've just heard about him. Not being a fan of his team, I never bother; I wasn't even a football fan, but seeing him like this makes me wish I had bothered to search for him on the internet more and see how he looked instead of just going over regular reports on him.

"Hey, are you okay?" he asks. I nodded my head, forcing a smile.

What's wrong with me? He is a client, and my gay ass is eyeing him like he's the last man in the world.

"Yes I'm fine, sorry just lack of caffeine. Would you like to start after your done getting dressed?" I asked him.

Not making eye contact, the last thing I need is a jock like him running out of the room yelling out fag.

My stomach let out a low growl, causing my face to get heated. I'm hoping he didn't hear that.

When he didn't answer, I looked back to find him walking near the kitchen, grabbing a plate and filling it with food.

I guess he's going to have something to eat before the interview then.

I watched him grab a coffee cup and fill it with coffee.

Jesse walked towards me; I avoided his eyes until he stood before me with the plate of food and coffee.

"Here, sit and eat on the island. I'm going to get dressed and meet you here afterward," he said, handing me the food.

I was about to say no thanks, but that look he gave me said I better accept the food.

I thanked him for the food and made my way to the seat in front of the island.

He stared at me for a bit before walking away into a room, which I assumed was the bedroom in the hotel suite.

My eyes wandered around the hotel room. It looks really expensive to stay here. They probably gave him one of their best rooms, considering who he is.

I looked at the plate in front of me and sighed. I hadn't had breakfast, so having breakfast now would be a lifesaver. I took some bites of the food on the plate and sipped some coffee.

I heard the door of the room he had walked into earlier open, but I didn't look up for some reason. I wasn't sure what the look on my face would be like.

Why am I attracted to him?

I've been so busy with work that I feel like this is because I haven't gotten any action lately.

By action, I mean watching videos online of hot men; I've never bothered going out there and getting the real deal myself.

"Well, you were really hungry. Look at how you're stuffing your mouth," he laughed. I stopped eating, took another sip of coffee, and prepared my notes.

"Hey, don't let me stop you. Eat more," Jesse said, sitting down next to me. I decided to lift my head to look at him, making sure to stare at him with a blank facial expression.

"Did you like the food? "he asked. I nodded my head and looked away from him, feeling embarrassed.

"It was really good," I said, thank you.

"Let's start," I said, grabbing my recorder and asking him questions from my notepad.

I sat down to interview him, asking him all the questions I had written; we were at our last question before I knew it, and Jesse was wrapping it up.

"Alright, we're done here. Thank you for your time, Mr.Hutcherman." I said, getting up and grabbing my things to get ready to leave.

"Jesse, you can call me Jesse," he said, smiling as he grabbed my plate and cup.

Oh shit, I should at least clean up after myself.

"Hey, I'm sorry I'm being rude. Do you need any help?" I asked him.

He looked up at me and started laughing.

"No, it's okay. It's one plate and a cup. I think I can manage." He said with a smirk as he walked towards the kitchen.

"Thank you for breakfast," I said.

"You're very welcome, Ben," he said, turning on the sink and washing the plate and cup.

The way he said my name sent a shiver down my body. I would love to hear him-

I stood there trying to figure out what was wrong with me. Why was I acting like this?

"You okay?" he asked, walking towards me. He put his hand on my forehead.

Great, now he was touching me. The last thing I needed right now was for him to touch me. He had these amazing green eyes, and I found myself staring into them.

"Yeah, I'm just tired, I guess," I said, pulling myself away from his touch and smiling as I nodded toward the door.

I walked towards the door, getting ready to leave until Jesse spoke.

"Hey! I'm new to this area and I really don't know anyone. I need someone to show me around are you free?" Jesse asked.

What?

Was he asking me to show him around?

Why doesn't he have someone hire someone to do that? But yet, I found myself answering to do it anyway.

"Yeah, sure, when?"I found myself asking as I turned around to face him.

A smile appeared on his face.

"Give me your number. Is tomorrow around 1:35 p.m. good for you? "he asked as we exchanged numbers.

"Sounds good," I said, walking away from him again and going towards the door. I heard him following close by, and a shiver ran down my back because of how close he was.

When I got to the door, I opened it and walked out.

"Bye, Jesse," I said, glancing back and waving.

He was staring at me with his phone as he smiled.

He waved back; I turned around and heard the door to his hotel room close.

When I entered the elevator, I felt a vibration coming from my phone when I glanced to see what it was. I noticed that it was a text message from Jesse.

"Hey, I can't wait for tomorrowo. Thank youu so much. Bye Ben." I found myself smiling at being able to see him again.

(*Kassandra Speaks*)

Aww, how cute are these two so far?

Chapter 2 Behave Boy

C hapter 2 Behave Boy

Ben POV

Today was my day off. I should have been relaxing, but I'll be showing the football Jesse Hutcherman around the city instead. The football player, who I know I am attracted to. The football player, I am sure, would not be interested in me or know I even see him that way.

I will have to make sure he doesn't see that I am attracted to him; at least I'll be able to be around him more. There may be more things that I could write about when it comes to him.

There's a lot to Jesse Hutcherman. I gathered that vibe yesterday when I interviewed him.

Call it a journalist feeling all you want, but he is hiding something, and I will find out what he's hiding. I got up from my bed and went to my bathroom.

I live in a condo, which fits my personality well, so when I saw it, you can say I became attached to it. I brushed my teeth and got in the shower.

When was the last time I went out? Some people say that I'm pretty dull. All I have been finding myself doing is work and coming home.

I don't even have a pet, but maybe that's how it was meant to be. Being a loner is not that bad, but I'm used to it. I've been a loner as long as I can remember. Switching from foster homes to foster homes, you learn that, honestly, no one cares about you in this world.

That no one gives a damn about you, that as soon as you think someone cares about you. They walk away, making you feel worthless and less human.

So I refused to go through that, so I don't have friends.

As depressing as it sounds, I don't want to get attached to anyone or have any feelings for anyone.

I don't want anyone to make me feel.

I'm a guy who doesn't believe in fairy tales or happily ever after.

Yet why am I even going out around the city with this football player?

My mind wandered to how he looked yesterday, and I found myself touching myself as memories of that day came into my mind.

"Jesse." I found myself moaning his name the whole time I was in the shower.

"Gosh, what's wrong with me?" I found myself saying out loud as I turned off the shower.

I never masturbated to any guy before. Why now?

I needed to control myself, I will be going around the city with Jesse today. This feeling that I am feeling for him needs to go away.

He will never be interested in me, and he's not going to see me that way either. I sighed and exited the shower, facing reality from the tingle of my daydream.

My phone was ringing. I answered it

"Hello?" I said

I looked at the time, and it was 12:35 p.m.

"Hey Ben, It's me, Jesse. I'm just making sure you didn't forget our plans today."

I looked in the mirror and saw that water was still dripping from my body from my shower with a lustful look on my face; he just had to call now?

"Of course not. I couldn't let football player Jesse Hutcherman walk around the city lost, could I now?" I heard him chuckling on the other end.

That chuckle alone brought a smile to my face. It sounded nice. "Yeah, you're right; that can't happen. I hate to see it on the news." He said.

"Make sure you're the first journalist to write about it. Also, don't forget to mention that it's your fault, too," he said, laughing.

I actually laughed. I don't know why, but it made me laugh.

"Woah, was that a laugh I heard?" he asked.

As I headed towards my closet.

"No, that was a cough," I said, I said laughing a little bit at my lame joke.

Well, I like the way you coughed then. Anyway, where do you want to meet?" he asked me.

I stopped doing what I was doing and stared at my phone, stunned.

Did he just say what I think he said?

Did he just say he likes the way I cough?

Calm down, Ben. You're taking a friendly gesture the wrong way.

He isn't flirting, right? No, it's not possible that he is.

"Or I can pick you up?" he quickly asked.

I didn't say anything for a few seconds, unsure if this man was just overly friendly or was actually flirting with me.

"Sure, I'll text you my address." I found myself taking a leap by giving a stranger my address to meet with me.

"Alright I'll bring us breakfast too, Bye," He said.

He hung up before I could say that it wasn't necessary for him to bring me breakfast.

My stomach let out a loud growl, objecting to my thoughts of it not being necessary. I sighed, texted Jesse my address, placed my phone on the dresser, and changed my thought process.

I went through my closet looking for something to wear and came up with a blue T-shirt and black jeans.

That should be good to wear for the day.

I looked at myself in the mirror and analyzed how I looked.

I like this shirt. Why have I never bothered wearing it until now?

When I looked at the time, it was 1:25 p.m.

"How the heck did it go by this fast?" I asked myself.

Leaving my bedroom, I headed towards the living room and grabbed a book. Before I could open my book, I heard a knock on my door.

That's definitely him. I stood up, feeling nervous about everything now—about what I was wearing and about how I was already envisioning this guy.

I walked towards my front door and unlocked it using the six door locks I had.

I kept my door extra locked, hoping it was something Jesse didn't ask about right now.

As that is something, I am uncomfortable with talking to someone about the reason behind it.

My eyes widened when I opened the door and found Jesse standing on the other side. How can he look that good? This guy is so fucking handsome.

"Hey, I know I'm early." I eyed him up and down. God help me; how am I going to behave today? My body was already starting to feel all flustered.

This man looks so good. I will have to be on my best behavior and keep things light.

(*Kassandra Speaks*)

Ben is obviously attracted to Jesse, but what about Jesse? Do you think he is attracted to Ben?

Chapter 3 is this a date?

C hapter 3: is this a date?

Ben Pov

"You okay?" he asked me as I gazed at him.

He asked if I was okay.

No, I was not okay.

I was trying to hold back and control all the emotions right now that were running through my body.

This was hard; I was a man, a gay man who had never felt or been attracted to anyone like this before, until him.

So, no, I was not okay. But I needed to be okay to get through this day. I need to be nice and friendly so everything can return to how it was before.

"Yeah I'm fine just didn't think you would be here so soon."

I said, avoiding his eyes and looking back at the clock. At 1:25 p.m., I turned around to find him smiling; I felt confused about why he kept staring at me and smiling.

My eyes widened when I realized I didn't invite him in.

"Do you want to come in until it's time to leave?" I said to him.

Jesse nodded, and I moved away from the door to let him in.

"Nice place you got here; it looks comfy," he said, smiling.

Jesse walked to the couch and sat down, still with a smile on his face. He placed the bag of food he was holding on the coffee table.

"Sure make yourself at home, Jesse," I said teasingly, taking even myself off guard.

I was not someone who normally behaved like that. I closed the front door and walked further into where Jesse sat.

"Can I get you anything? It's the least I can do from what you did for me yesterday—giving me food and stuff." I said, not knowing what to say.

"Haha, you're funny, yeah. If you don't mind, I'm kind of hungry. I would like a sandwich and a glass of juice." He said, playfully looking at the food bag on the coffee table.

I didn't know how long I stood there staring at him, and I don't know which one got me the most.

Jesse is laughing at my lame joke or giving me that smile that has my heart beating.

"You want me to make you a sandwich?" I asked him, shaking my head and heading towards my kitchen after grabbing the bag of food he brought in off the coffee table.

"Yes, please! Can I watch some TV also? Since you told me to make myself at home," he said with a chuckle.

I rolled my eyes and nodded, letting him know it was fine.

I took some of the food out of the containers and placed them on the plates I took out. I realized that I was smiling.

What's going on with me? Why am I even smiling like this?

I am in my kitchen, preparing a plate of food for myself and this football player I met yesterday for the first time. Who happens to be sitting down and watching TV in my living room.

Yet, I didn't mind doing this because I wanted to, and the strange thing is I had a feeling that made me feel that I could see myself doing this more often.

This shocked me. I shook my thoughts away and braced myself to appear in front of Jesse again.

After putting the food on the plate, I went to the fridge and grabbed a gallon of apple juice to pour into each cup.

I placed it back in the fridge, took a straw from my straw cup, and put it in the cup of juice. I grabbed the plate with the sandwich, grabbed the cup, and started heading towards the living room.

When I reached the living room, I saw Jesse staring at me. Feeling strangely undressed by his eyes, I avoided eye contact and placed the sandwich and drink on the coffee table before him.

"Your meal is ready, sir," I said. He didn't reply, so I figured what I said annoyed him, but when I looked up, I saw him giving me a smirk.

"Thank you; I appreciate it." He said as he took his plate.

He grabbed his sandwich and took a bite; his eyes widened.

"Mmm, this is really good, this is so good," he said, taking another bite. I laughed as I sat down to eat the sandwich as well.

It was delicious, and I would have to ask him where he picked up the food.

"So you ready to see the big city?" I asked him, sounding like a teacher taking a child on a field trip.

He nodded his head while eating his sandwich. I looked at him well; he looked good today and comfortable.

"Yeah! I'm pretty excited. As I mentioned, it's my first time being here, and I didn't want to just sit around and do nothing." He said, drinking his juice and taking a napkin from the coffee table. I understood what he meant by that.

There was no point in not exploring a place you would be visiting or staying in to see what the place offers.

We both continued eating and chatting with each other about random things. When we were both done, I stood up and stretched.

He quickly held on to it as I was about to grab his plate. "I can wash my own plate, you know." He said, causing me to hold back a laugh.

Was he doing it on purpose? Joking?

I looked at him and gave him a smirk. He looked confused about why I was smiling at him, but then I could see when it dawned on him, and he started laughing.

"Ha, who would have thought, well, alright then? Guess I deserve that."

I chuckled and walked away. Knowing he would say something, I speed-walked into my kitchen. "Was that a laugh I heard Ben?"

There was something about the way he said my name.

It felt like he saying it as if it was the most important thing to him.

I shook my head and stopped when I reached the sink, knowing he couldn't see me shaking my head. "No. There was something in my throat." I said in a joking tone. This was going to be something that was just our thing, something that we would find ourselves doing with each other.

I found myself stopping myself from thinking such a thing; he and I would most likely only hang out for today. I don't know why I even had that thought in the first place.

I washed our plates and cups, drying them and putting them away.

"Ready to go?" I asked, walking towards the coat rack to grab my coat.

"So you live alone?" Jesse asked, getting up.

I turned around to face him, lifting a brow to the question he asked.

"Yeah, it's just me. It's common though." I said to him

"Do you like living alone?" He asked.

I froze.

I didn't expect that question and didn't even know how to answer it.

"Ben?" He said.

He called my name and brought my attention back to him; he had a concerned look on his face.

"Sorry for asking. I was just being nosey," he said, coming closer to me. I found myself backing away from each step he took.

We played this little dance until I found myself leaning on the wall. Jesse walked up to me and stared down at me. Now that he was this close to me, I noticed he was taller than me. I could smell him. He was wearing this really lovely cologne, and I found myself getting addicted to the way it smelled.

"Ben?" Jesse said; I didn't look up at him and continued to stare at where his collarbone was.

I was afraid to look up at him, to make eye contact with him because if I did, there would be no way I could mask my attraction to him. He had me cornered, and I had no idea why he was standing in front of me or why I was against the wall.

"Hey, Sunshine." He said, causing me to look up at him with wide eyes.

Sunshine? What? Why did he call me that?

He raised his hand and moved a piece of my hair that fell on my forehead.

He was touching me.

I held my breath as Jesse made direct eye contact with me.

He backed away from me and smiled while opening the door.

"I'm ready, let's go." He said, holding the door open for me.

I was confused; what did he just do? What was that?

I turned to face him, but Jesse still stared at me, waiting for me to walk out the door.

I didn't even know what to say. This was my first time going on a date with anyone.

Wait, what did I just think? This isn't a date, Ben. You're just showing him around.

Get that through your head; no one will ever be interested in you that way.

This guy isn't attracted to you like you're attracted to him.

I pushed back my thoughts and walked towards the front door.

This wasn't the time, but why did he do that?

I looked up at him, confused about what had happened. Was he not going to talk about it? About him calling me sunshine?

"Where do you want to go first?" I asked him, walking out the front door.

My voice came out raspy, and I cleared my throat. I was surprised that I sounded like that.

I turned to face Jesse, he closed the front door and waited for me to lock it.

I asked him again.

"Where do you want to go first?" I said, not making eye contact with him; Jesse leaned over me, his mouth next to my ear, taking me off guard.

"I'll go wherever you want to go," he said, sending a shiver down my back.

It's safe to say he is flirting with me now.

Right?

(* Kassandra speaks*)

I finally updated!!!!!!!!! Ugh, I can't believe that it took this long! Of course, I didn't forget about my babies. I love them so much; I love all my babies. Yes, I finally uploaded it, but hey. Gay marriage has been legalized in 50 states! So why not update this beautiful story that will have you lusting for me??? This was a short chapter, but I'm going to spice it up on the next one!!!!!! Yes, Lol. Feel free to follow my social media and subscribe to my YouTube channel. Bye dolls Ciao Xoxoxoxo –Kassandra Vivu

Chapter 4 He's Different

Chapter 4 He's different.

BEN POV

We were walking around the city now; we decided to take an Uber to stop from place to place without worrying about where we parked.

Jesse surprised me with his energy, as he had questions about everything. Jesse asked questions as we toured the city, from the landscapes and historical monuments to the new constructions. He wanted to know about it all. Jesse wanted to know every single detail. It was as if he was a kid on a field trip.

How did I get stuck doing this? I don't remember how, but I didn't mind. Seeing a football player's face get excited just from me telling him about things in the city was funny.

"You know Jesse for a football player; you sure don't act like one." I mentioned as we continued our walk.

He looked at me and started laughing.

"Oh, really Ben? How is a football player supposed to act?" He asked with a raised brow.

I gave him a confused look as if it wasn't obvious.

"Like jocks," I said in a low tone; it was no surprise that football players were known to be jocks.

I have never heard about a football player with a dork side or a real dork side.

He stopped walking and stared at me as if to say, 'Are you serious?'

"Wow Ben, isn't that high school mentallity." Jesse said with a look of humor on his face.

I shook my head sure some of it was from experience dealing with stuff in high school, but that doesn't mean that the statement doesn't somehow hold.

"Nope," I said, making sure I popped the P and kept walking. He started walking again just to keep up with me.

"How were you like in high school? Since I'm the jock." Jesse asked, catching up to me.

How was I in high school? I didn't even want to answer that question.

I didn't have a good time in high school and hated remembering anything related to that time.

He stopped; I continued walking and realized that Jesse was no longer following close behind me.

When I turned around, I found him still standing and not moving.

"Aren't you coming?" I asked him

"Not until you tell me which kid you were in high school," he said, with a serious, determined look on his face.

I shook my head as I looked at the stubborn football player.

He was definitely a jock.

"I was an outcast," I said, shrugging my shoulders.

I continued walking away but heard footsteps behind me; Jesse took hold of my arm and pulled me gently towards him.

"What do you mean you were an outcast?" he asked.

Staring at me, I could only think about this hand still holding onto my arm.

"I was an outcast, had no friends. Never did, spoke to no one, had everyone thinking what was up with me. I was a loner and still am. It wasn't something that I minded though, it was what it was." I said, removing my arm from his hold.

This conversation was heading a way I didn't want it to.

"Ben.... surely you had someone?" Jesse asked, still staring at me.

"No Jesse, I honestly had no one in high school. No one bother getting to know me. No one bother caring for me or being in my life I had no one. Maybe it was meant to be like that. I ended up being okay, I mean we all have our issues here and there, but I'm still fine." I said, wanting to avoid the conversation more now.

I sounded so freaking sad saying that out loud; I didn't feel sad, but the way Jesse was staring at me made me feel like what I was saying was something pathetic.

I felt him grab me by the side and turn me around. Why was he doing all of this?

This guy is very touchy. Was this a football player thing? To be this touchy, especially with someone you just met?

He didn't say anything; a minute or two passed, and Jesse still didn't speak.

I still haven't made direct eye contact with him, but his not saying anything or moving bothered me.

"Jesse, let's keep doing this tour, okay? We're wasting time," I said to him, my tone serious. Whatever he was doing was wasting both our time.

"Would you let me be that person?" Jesse asked.

Huh? What? What is he talking about?

"What?" I asked out loud.

"Would you let me be that person?" He asked in a gentle tone.

I looked up at him, making eye contact to find a raw look on his face.

I didn't know what to say; how Jesse stared made me squirm.

"What are you even talking about?" I asked, sounding breathless. What was wrong with me? Why does this guy get me this way?

"Let me in your life, I want to be in it." He said, pulling me into a hug.

Did he forget that we were out in about?

I was going to say something until I felt his heartbeat against his chest.

He's hugging me; he says he wants to be in my life.

What is it that this guy wants? And why do I like it this much?

*******Kassandra Speaks*******

Aw, things get cute things get cute,

I love Jesse's personality and was so surprised I wrote about him. I'm so proud of myself; they're all my children.

Something juicy happens in the next chapter, but let's ask the important questions, shall we? Will Ben let Jesse in?

Is Jesse even straight?

Why does Ben think all football players are the same? Does he have something against them?

In the meantime, Vote, Comment, and Follow. Thanks, Dolls.

Chapter 5 How did this happen?

C hapter 5 How did this Happen?

Ben Pov

Does he even know what he's asking?

Is this because he feels bad for me?

I don't need anyone feeling bad for me; like I mentioned, I'm okay.

"Um, how about no?" I said. Shaking my head on how weird this guy could be.

"Aw, come on, we could be friends." He said.

Oh, friends, that's what he meant; of course, that's what he would mean. Why did I think he could have meant something more?

Did I actually want him to mean it another way? I don't even know myself.

This feeling that I am feeling is all new for me.

He thinks that we could be friends?

There's no way we could be friends because I am already attracted to him.

"Sure, Jesse. We can try to be that." I said to him; he looked relieved. A smile appeared on his face.

I still do not know what else to say.

I wanted something more than friendship, but that is not allowed.

He doesn't want that after all.

"Where do you want to go anyways? Like what do you want to see around this area? You can't tell me you want me to show you around and not tell me what you want to see Jesse. It doesn't work out like that." I said to him.

He chuckled and shrugged as if what I said was not a big deal. I picked up the pace again, and Jesse caught up with me. I decided to walk steadily.

"You know I want to go anywhere you want to go," he said, and I rolled my eyes. Fine, he wants to play this game. Fine, we can play this game.

"Let's go to my favorite park," I said, looking up at him; damn him for being so tall.

"We can do that, do we have to take another uber or?" Jesse asked.

It was pretty close from here.

"We could walk there; it isn't that far from here at all," I said, knowing how to get from the park from here.

"Okay sounds good." He said as we continued walking.

"Sooo... what's your favorite color?" He asked me.

What's up with that question?

"Gold." I replied.

He stared at me with amusement in his eyes.

"Gold?" he asked, and I nodded.

What's wrong with liking gold?

"What's yours?" I asked him.

"Black," he said with a smile on his face.

I stopped walking and looked at him.

His favorite color was black? Yet he found humor in me liking gold?

"I like the shade black. When you stare at a black wall for too long, you notice that it's actually changing. That it's letting you in." He said, I raised a brow to that. I never thought of it that way.

"We've reached the park," I said when we got to where the entrance would be.

"I'll show you my favorite spot," I said, leading him in.

"So is this where you come, Ben, when you want to escape the chaotic world?" He asked.

I turned my attention toward him, and I found myself feeling odd. Honestly, this was the first time I have ever brought anyone here.

"Yes," I said, but it came as a whisper.

"But this is my favorite spot," I said, standing in front of the spot I love to come to. It was in front of a lake surrounded by trees, the most beautiful scene in the park.

I walked ahead, enjoying the view. I could never get tired of this beautiful view. It just brings me to ease every single time I see it.

"Wow, the view is beautiful. I could get used to this," he said, and I nodded, agreeing. I turned around to tell him how I found this place, but I found him standing right behind me, staring at me.

I felt my heartbeat and saw the look he was giving me. Wait, I'm reading too much into this, right?

Maybe he found it amusing that I can get like this over this place?

"Am I blocking the view for you?" I asked, planning to move out of the way so he could see what I saw.

"You're part of the view." Jesse said. His voice held no humor.

I felt myself getting heated up.

Why is he saying things like that?

"Don't say that." I said, wrapping my arms around me.

"Don't say what?" he asked, walking towards me.

"Don't say stuff like that; it confuses me even more," I said, looking at him.

Why was he coming closer?

"Confuses you about what?" He asked, standing in front of me.

"It makes me feel like you're flirting with me or something, it's confusing me." I said, avoiding his gaze.

I felt him wrap his arms around me and pull me into a hug.

He's being touchy again.

"You seem to have forgotten what I said earlier. I want to get to know you more. If it makes you feel any better, we can start as friends, and I have been flirting with you from day one. I want to be in your life, Ben. I want to be around you. So, there's no way I am going to stop saying stuff like that, especially not with you," he said, kissing my forehead.

What did he just say?

Did he really just say that?

"Are you gay?" I asked, pulling away to look at him.

"I'm not gay, but I know that I am attractive to you. You're the first guy I have ever been attracted to. I also want to say what I have been feeling for you is new for me, I've never felt this way for anyone I've ever been involved with either. It's new for me, something that I wasn't expecting. But I want to try this; I know I want to be with you. So I'm asking you to let me be in your life. I'm not going to beat around the bush about it." He said, his tone serious.

Can I do this? Can I let him into my life? A loner like me, who's never been involved with anyone like this before. Can I learn to trust someone and let him in?

"What do you say Ben?" Jesse whispers.

"Okay." I found myself saying it, not knowing the relief I felt after I said it myself.

Jesse smiled immediately after hearing my response.

"Thank you, Ben."

Kassandra Speaks

WOAH! It's been good

I love this couple.

I mean, they're my babies.

Haha, I love them.

Anyway, this story has been the bomb even though I am slow

with updates.

CURSE YOU SCHOOL AND HAVING A LIFE

But I will update my Dolls soon.

Enjoy mwah

Xoxoxo-Kassandra Vivu

Happy Holidays to you!

Chapter 6 What did I get into

Chapter 6 What did I get into?

Ben POV

"So, let's get to know each other better," Jesse said as he sat beside me.

We were sitting in front of the lake now.

"Okay, we can do that," I said, still getting used to our current vibe.

Jesse confessed that he was interested in me in that way. After all that thinking, there's no way he would be interested in me.

I need a minute to gather all my thoughts.

"Tell me something that you consider a little dorky about yourself." I asked, curious to know what this man considered dorky.

He looked at me with a soft smile.

"I watch anime." He said, causing my eyes to widen.

"What? You do?" I asked him

"Yeah, and I really like it a lot. I've been watching it since I was five years old, and you kind of remind me of this anime character I used to like—he was sort of this dark prince character." He said a tint of red could be seen on his cheek.

"I also read manga, I like collecting volumes of them." He said, shrugging.

I stayed quiet, not able to say anything.

Jesse looked at me and asked.

"Is it weird or something to you?" Jesse said with a curious look.

"No, I also watch anime and read manga as well." I said, knowing that I was blushing.

Jesse let out a laugh, smiling from ear to ear.

"Love to hear it." He said, amused.

Who would have thought that we had something in common?

I turned my attention to Jesse and found him staring at me intensely.

"So what do you want to see now?" I asked, standing up. I was trying to figure out what to make of the look he was giving me.

"I'm finally kind of hungry." He said, getting up.

"We can go to a restaurant if you want," I said.

"Actually." He said, looking at me.

"I say we go back to your place, order some takeout and find a anime together to watch." he said with a sly smirk.

What?

He wants us to watch anime together?

The idea did sound nice.

I wouldn't mind being home right now and watching anime. But the problem is, I never had anyone spend time with me in my home. Things like him showing up at my place made me not know what to do. He was there earlier, but that was only for a short period.

Now he wants to supposedly watch anime with me and order takeout at my place.

"Are you sure that's what you really want to do?" I asked him, ensuring he wasn't just saying all of that because of me. The last thing I need is for someone to pity me.

"Oh yeah, we've toured quite a bit already; that's what I really want to do. Honestly, don't worry. I'm pretty blunt. I'll only ever say things that I mean." He said, smiling.

"Okay, I guess we should head back now," I said, walking back to where we came from with Jesse beside me.

"So besides watching anime, what else do you like to do?" He said as he walked next to me.

I glanced at him. He still wanted to get to know me better.

"I like painting and drawing," I said in a low voice.

That must have to perk his interest.

"Really? That's mad cool." He said.

"Thank you," I said as we reached the park exit.

"I know this is going to sound weird, but I want to actually get you to open up to me." He said as we started crossing the street with everyone else exiting the park.

"What do you mean?" I asked him as we reached the sidewalk, wondering why he even cared if I opened up.

"I want to know a lot about you, like things that interest you and those that don't, things that annoy you, and things that you like," he said, shrugging.

"Why, there's nothing special about it. Some of the things I like might be boring to you. ," I said.

"I don't think anything about you is boring. Hold on, let me get us an uber." Jesse said, taking out his phone.

"Also, let me be the judge of that sunshine." He said.

Why is he even calling me that?

I debated asking him the reason why he called me that but decided not to.

The Uber came, and we both got in, heading towards my condo.

I noticed that the uber driver was only making one stop, so he was serious about coming to my condo to watch anime with me.

We reached the condo building, got out, and thanked the Uber for the ride.

I avoided eye contact with Jesse. As we reached my condo door, I opened it to let him in, but I continued to avoid his eyes.

I could tell he was staring at me.

"Hey, Ben, listen. If you don't want me to stay and watch anime with you, it's fine. Honestly, I can leave if I'm invading your space," Jesse said.

I was trying to find the right words to say; it's not like I wanted him to leave or had an issue with spending time with him. I just knew I was going to be a nervous wreck.

"Okay, I got it. Bye, Ben. Thanks for the day, by the way. I had a good time." As he approached the door, I immediately grabbed his arm to stop him.

Jesse turned and stared at me; I finally raised my head and stared back at him.

"Don't leave... you can stay with me," I said, my voice coming out in a whisper.

Which didn't shock me at all. What surprised me was the smile on Jesse's face when he squeezed my hand and said,

"That's all I want." He said, smiling.

Kassandra Speaks

Finally Updated for this story, I will be working really hard on this story. It's so cute.

Ben is a wallflower who doesn't have anyone ever paying attention to him.

Until Jess came by when all of this was new to him.

Jess also wants Ben to let him in, which is bold and admirable.

Not many people would care like that or even try to understand someone like that, but Jesse is trying.

The next Chapter gets really good!!!

Stay tuned, dolls!!!!

#TeamBessie

XOXOXO

CH. 7 Who would have thought

C H. 7 Who would have thought

(Jesse POV)

I was surprised a lot today by many things.

One of them was what I was doing now; I was on the couch watching anime with another guy.

I enjoy watching anime, and this is the first time I have encountered someone who enjoys it as much as I do now.

Who would have thought that Jesse Hutcherman was intrigued by another man and was watching anime with him?

I turned to look at Ben sitting next to me on the couch.

We were watching an anime called Death Note, and I was trying to understand the plot and the concept of the anime while watching it.

"So, if he writes the name of a person name in the book, they die?" I asked Ben, trying to get an answer to my confusion.

"Yes. The person whose name he writes in the book dies as soon as he finishes writing their name." Ben said, eyes glued to the T.V. screen.

"How the hell do they die anyway?" I asked Ben again, who turned his attention back to me.

"The book is basically an evil demon book from hell, Jesse, so it's powered and basically causes the death of whoever name is written in it," Ben said.

"I'm also trying not to give you spoils on certain stuff." He said, causing me to run my eyes playfully.

I knew Ben was picking up on the fact that I craved getting spoiler alerts here and there, and he was unwilling to give me any.

"You think this anime is dumb don't you?" Ben asked me with a smirk.

I laughed at the look on his face.

"No, I just really like spoilers that's the only reason why I am asking so many questions.." I said.

"Yeah, I can tell." He said with a goofy look on his face.

"Did you want to pause watching Death Note and pick an anime? One I haven't seen but you have?" He asked me, pausing the episode we were on.

"No, we don't have to. It's okay." I said, not wanting him to stop watching an anime he enjoys.

"No, it's alright with me, it's an anime I've already watched and I am interested to see what kind of anime you'll pick for us to watch together." He said, giving me a challenging look.

Ben handed me the remote, and I took it from him, smiling.

I teased him about picking the best anime that would blow his mind.

He playfully rolled his eyes at that and scoffed. It was as if there was no way I could beat him with that.

I liked our little teasing, which meant we were getting comfortable with each other.

As I went through different options, I picked the one I knew would have him hooked.

"Attack on Titan," I said out loud, turning my head to stare at Ben to see if he approved.

He raised a brow at me. "I've never watched it, but I've read that it's pretty interesting. So why not?" he said, facing the T.V. again.

"Oh yeah, it's interesting, alright," I said, knowing that I had been watching the series and reading the manga. Attack on Titan is a show you have to prepare to watch. That's for sure, but I was interested to see what he would think of it.

I honestly had many things going through my mind at that very moment

I already knew I was falling for him; it was apparent that I was.

I wouldn't say I was Gay or Bi because he is the only guy I've found myself attracted to, and especially the only person I am attracted to right now.

I knew I was into him, but what could I do?

He made it evident that I wasn't his type. I don't think I'm his type. The way he talks about the Jock type and football players in general just shows that he wouldn't be interested in getting involved with one in that way.

I wanted to ask him what he would think of me in that way, and I wanted him to know that I was interested in him in that way.

I don't know the best way to ask him that.

So, I turned around and continued watching the anime with him, glancing at his facial expression whenever a scene popped up that I knew he would react to. I enjoyed those moments each time.

3 hours later

"Jesse, I think we've watched enough of this." I heard Ben.

I let out a laugh, not knowing what else to say. Three hours had passed, but I wanted to continue invading his space and watching more anime.

"Jesse," Ben said, catching my attention. In my best Titan behavior, I turned my head around slowly to stare at Ben.

"Ugh, don't do that. That's creepy. Don't ever do that again," Ben said with a horrified look; I chuckled at his facial expression.

"Alright, Ben, I'm down for us to binge this season, but if you have something to do. I can leave if you want me to?" I asked him, standing up and stretching.

I felt and heard my bones crack, giving me that great sense of feeling. A good stretch is always needed.

"I was wondering if you were hungry?" He asked me with a shy expression.

I was hungry; it's been a while since we ate, and I genuinely forgot about eating while watching the anime.

"Yes, I am for sure hungry. Are you offering to cook for me?" I said with a smirk on my face.

Ben got up and rolled his eyes. "I'll be in the kitchen." He says, getting up and walking towards the kitchen

I found my eyes lingering on Ben's retreating body.

I followed him into the kitchen, noticing that he was taking things out of the cabinets.

"What do you have in mind of making?" I asked him, interested in what he was going to make.

"Well, I'm going to make a baked chicken alfredo. Are you down for that?" He asked, walking towards the fridge and taking out some chicken.

I stilled, a smile appearing on my face. I was a sucker for a good chicken alfredo.

"Yeah, I'm good with that. It's actually my favorite." I said to him.

"That's great, it's mine also." He said, perking my attention.

As I watched Ben prepare the things he needed, my stare moved to the lip he was biting.

That did something to me, I don't know what it was or why, but I found a turn-on for him biting his lip.

I found myself walking towards Ben, who looked up confusedly.

It dawned on me earlier today that Ben had no idea how attractive he was, which blew my mind.

I stood before him, and he continued staring at me. I lifted my hand and rubbed a finger against his bottom lip, which alarmed Ben. He stared at me with wide eyes and a wary look.

"Can I kiss you?" I asked him.

"What?" He asked in a whisper.

"I want to kiss you, can I kiss you?" I said, making eye contact with him.

"Please," I said.

My voice sounded parched, I had no idea why, but all I wanted to do now was have my lips against his.

"Okay." Be said, and immediately as soon as he said that, I closed the distance between us and slammed my lips against his.

I groaned as I ran my fingers through his hair, the same hair I had been staring at the whole day.

I don't know if it was because he was shocked, but it took a while for Ben to start responding to my kiss, and when he did, I couldn't hold back the eagerness of wanting to twirl my tongue with his.

I pushed my tongue against his lips, asking for entrance, and a groan came from me again when Ben opened his mouth gently.

God kissing him felt amazing; touching him felt amazing.

Ben let out a whimper; it was the sexiest thing I've ever heard.

I moved my lips from his and trailed kisses down his neck.

I immediately felt Ben's fingers through my hair, which got me even hotter.

The kisses I was trialing down Ben's neck became me sucking on it. The noises that were coming from him were driving me crazy.

I want Ben in every way. I want him to be mine, I want to be in a relation-ship with him, and I want us to start dating. I felt a little nerve-wracking because this was all new for me, but I wanted it.

"I want you. All of you," I said to him. It was like a switch had been turned on. Ben immediately pulled out of my arms and distanced himself; he immediately ran out of the kitchen.

Kassandra Speaks

Woah, this chapter is interesting; my characters are getting closer and closer to each other.

Why did Ben run out of the kitchen?

The next chapter gets interesting.

It's exciting; until then, stay tuned. But Hey, comment, what do you think will happen next!!

SO here's the stitch

H ello my lovely beautiful Dolls, how're you Dolls, my lovely Goddesses and Gods doing?

Good? well, I hope so.

So I wanted to let you all know something that has been bothering me lately.

I notice that the views I've been getting on my stories don't match up to the amount of VOTES, FOLLOWING DOLLS & COMMENTS.

I mean I did try not let it bother me but it sorta knocks down the walls and found its way in.

For example, I would get so many views on a chapter but barely any VOTES, COMMENTS, AND People who read the chapters didn't even follow.

Don't get me wrong, I love My DOLLS!!! LOVE THEM. You guys are extremely amazing supporters and I love you all!!!

It's just the people who leave me rude comments and message me rudely asking why I haven't updated but they're not even a Doll.

Like they're not even following me, or voting on my stories but demanding these things from me.

I don't keep anything from you DOLLS, I don't even see you guys as a Fan base but Members of a book CLUB which I like to call DOLLS.

That's why I call you DOLLS, I love that you guys enjoy my stories which boost me to write more.

Reason, why updates are so late, is because

I'm becoming a TEACHER, to grade school kids. (DO I want to do this forever? No my field of study is Criminal justice, criminal Law, and social psychology.

I'm making some work down to MY YOUTUBE CHANNEL AND WEBSITES.

So those of you who didn't know I had a channel I do.

My youtube is Kassandravivu

Youtube.com/Kassandravivu

It would make me happy if you go on it and hit that subscribe button, I will begin posting videos Late May or Early June.

I'm going to school for Criminal justice, Law, Culinary and Design Fundamentals. (Which will come in handy you'll see)

I'm starting my OWN BRAND OF PRODUCTS WHICH I WILL BEGIN SELLING AROUND JUNE!!!!

So Dolls these are reasons why I'm late with Updates. This Queen Doll has Goals!!!!!

Love you all! and to the GHOST VIEWERS, STOP BEING A GHOST AND HIT THAT FOLLOW BUTTON AND VOTE AND COMMENT ON MY STORIES.

Instagram , Twitter, Snapchat: Kassandravivu

GOING TO LOVE UPDATING THIS STORY

Ch. 8 He doesn't mean it. Right?

CH. 8 He doesn't mean it. Right?

(Ben POV)

I rushed to my room, stunned about what had just happened.

What in the world was that? I asked myself.

Did he just say that? Did he mean that? I looked around my room in confusion. He kissed me, and I kissed him back.

I touched my lips; the kiss that happened between us was something that I liked a lot. Yet, it was something that was not supposed to happen.

I can't do things like that with people I interviewed.

Why did he kiss me? Why did I even allow him to kiss me? I mean, he asked for consent, and I said it was okay, but part of me was wondering if he would do it.

Is he attracted to me?

I didn't have to look in the mirror to know that my face was already red, but I couldn't help the butterflies that I was feeling.

He kissed me for a reason; he asked to kiss me for a reason.

He wanted to kiss me, and I ran out of the kitchen as soon as he finished.

Gosh, what is wrong with me? I'm a whole nervous wreck.

I left the bedroom and found Jesse standing right where I left him, still. He didn't even move; it was as if he was frozen.

Running away after the kiss was something that I shouldn't have done.

This was new to both of us, especially to him, and here I am causing us both to be nervous about it even more.

"Jesse," I said, walking towards him. He turned to face me, a confused look on his face.

I didn't know what to say, but Jesse cut me off before I could even come up with anything.

"Why did you run out? Did I do something wrong? I'm sorry if I made you uncomfortable but I was serious when I said I like you and I'm attracted to you." He said, staring at me.

"I'm sorry it was unexpected, and I just didn't think you would do that. Honestly, Jesse, I don't know what to think of this. I honestly just don't want to be someone's experiment to see if they like men or not. I'm honestly too fragile to get hurt like that, Jesse, and if that's what you're looking for, then you found the wrong person because I can't deal with that." I said, meaning every word.

"I didn't kiss you because I was experimenting. I kissed you because the level of attraction I felt for you was already there." He said in a severe tone.

He pinched the bridge of his nose, let out a sigh, and then spoke.

"I want you, I like you and I am attracted to you. You're not an experiment to see if I am gay or not. Honestly, I don't think I am gay but I know I am feeling a lot of crazy emotions right now for you and I don't see this feeling going away. Also, I'm not going to keep you a secret. if you give me a chance to show you that. I will, I don't care who knows. You're definitely someone worth bragging about." Jesse said, staring at me with raw emotions.

I let his words settle in. I would be lying if I didn't admit that the level of pull and attraction I felt towards him wasn't there, but what was scary to me was that we had just met and were already feeling this way towards each other.

"You like me, seriously? No games?" I asked him. He walked towards me, pulled me into his arms, and kissed me again.

My heart was slamming against my chest as Jesse continued to kiss me.

I wanted to touch him, so I decided to. I ran my fingers through his hair, lightly tugging him closer to me, wanting to deepen the kiss even more.

We pulled back from each other, both of us catching our breaths. When I made direct contact with Jesse, the way his eyes looked and the look on his face confirmed to me that he was serious about all of this.

A soft smile appeared on my face.

"I am very serious about this, Ben, I'm already addicted to kissing you and even want to do it again right now, especially when you have that look on your face," Jesse said in a flustered tone.

"What look?" I asked him as he kissed my forehead; my eyelids fluttered close from the affectionate feeling I was receiving.

He pulled back and lowered his gaze to match mine. "That cute look you have on your face whenever I kiss you as if you just received a gift that you have been waiting for a long time," he said, smiling.

I stared at him. He was very handsome, and I'm sure everyone noticed.

I couldn't help; my hand reached his face as I softly rubbed my thumb on his right cheek. Jesse leaned against the touch.

"You're so beautiful, so handsome," I said.

" You're one to talk. You have no idea how attractive and stunning you look. I am going to make you see that. But I seem to remember your promise to cook for me Before you ran away from our first kiss, a kiss I enjoyed very much." Jesse said in a teasing tone.

"Sorry about that, I was just very nervous, but yes, you're right, I did promise to cook for you. So I will get to it." I said, smiling.

"It's okay to be nervous. I mean, I was nervous kissing you, too," he said, rubbing the back of his head.

I felt a tug on my heart as I stared at Jesse.

"Would you like to have something on as I cook?" I asked him.

"Sure, that's fine. Do you have any recommendations on what I should have?" he asked me as I moved around in the kitchen.

"Hmm, anything. You can even put on a horror movie if you want." I suggested to him.

"Scary movie, huh?" he asked, a little stunned.

"Yes, scary movie, and a good one, too, not any of those bad ones that just don't make sense," I said, teasing him.

"Jesse," I said his name seriously.

"What is it that you want between us?" I asked him, lowering my gaze to look at my fingers. For some reason, at that very moment, I found my fingers interesting to look at.

"I would like us to get to know each other more, to start dating, to become boyfriends and of course, I am looking for even more after that." He said, taking me off guard about what he could have meant by that.

"Hmm, well I do want to have that too, but I also want a strong friendship behind that. I meant what I said about not having a lot of people in my life. So, I would want us to be great friends, best friends during those stages as well." I said.

Relationships don't last if people can't be friends during it.

Jesse approached me and lifted my head so that our stares matched.

"You got it, baby." He said; I knew from the way my face was starting to heat up that I was red, and Jesse, of course, confirmed that with the smile that appeared on his face.

"Baby?" I asked.

"Mhm, I'm going to be calling you that a lot now. I really would like to." He said, pressing a kiss on my cheek.

"Feel free to call me anything you like," he said, kissing my neck and causing shivers throughout my whole body.

"Okay," I said softly.

Jesse pulled back; he stared at me as if he wanted to say or do something.

"Shit, Ben. Yeah, you have no idea how fucking attractive you look." He said, letting out a chuckle.

"Yeah, I am attracted to you in every way, no more doubting that okay?" He asked.

"Okay." That was all I could muster to say because I was definitely very attracted to him in every way, too.

Kassandra Speaks

It looks like Jesse is serious about him and Ben. Poor Ben thought Jesse was most likely just using it as an experiment, but Jesse checked him real quick about that. Hmm, why would Ben think of that? Does it mean something from his past happened like that to him before?

I love how open Jesse is, don't you? He basically told Ben that he never felt like that with anyone else until he met him. Let's see how these feelings work out. Give this story a voice, comment, and share!!! CHECK OUT MY OTHER BOOKS TOO. Love you dolls!!

xoxoxo

-Kassandra Vivu

Ch. 9 Never Felt this

G if of Ben found above

Ch. 9 Never felt this

(Jesse POV)

What can I say? I had the chance to kiss him, so I took it, and I damn well have never felt that way before.

When he ran out, I honestly felt my heart clenched.

I didn't want to scare him, but the chance was there, so I had to take it. I also asked if it was okay with him, although Ben said yes. I know he ran the way he did because he was still nervous.

I've never ever been with a man before, and I've kissed plenty of girls.

Those girls had nothing on the kisses I just had with Ben.

I could hear Ben moving around in the kitchen while I sat on the couch, searching for a horror movie on the T.V.

I would be okay with this becoming something I would find myself doing often.

When he told me he didn't have any friends and had never been in any form of relationship.

That hit me and urged me to prove I would be his friend. Heck, I'll be his best friend, and I damn well want to be in a relationship with him.

I decided to steal some glances at Ben in the kitchen; he looked cute while cooking.

The fact that this man is so cute.

I turned around and looked through the horror movie options on the T.V. to see what I could find.

I saw a movie called The Poltergeist and noticed it was released in 1982. After reading the summary, I decided to go with it.

I hope he liked the choice of the movie I picked.

When I was told I would be interviewed by a journalist, I didn't think much about it, but when I saw him, for some reason, I found myself wanting to get to know him.

I haven't been this happy in a long time. My mother always told me to hold onto anything that made me happy and giddy. I knew that I wanted to hold onto Ben.

I wanted to know him, his likes and dislikes, favorite colors and foods, and what he wanted but had yet to do.

I felt a lot of things for Ben; it was insane because we had just met.

Yet, it felt very right, and I would be a fool not to act on these feelings.

Ben was making me feel that way. I would not run away from something like this or be too scared to pursue it. No, I was going to do the opposite. I want to pursue what I felt with Ben because I knew he felt the same way.

Although I was shocked that he ran away after I kissed him, it was like it was his first kiss or something.

I was happy that he allowed it again, especially seeing the emotions on his face.

I was so lost in thoughts that I didn't even know he was done cooking and placing the food on the coffee table until he spoke.

"I see you picked the Poltergeist. Nice choice, it's an old movie but I think you might like it if you haven't seen it." He said while he sat down next to me.

My eyes widened, realizing that he was next to me.

I turned to face him and smiled.

"So you've seen it before? Are you okay with seeing it again?" I asked Ben.

"Yes, it's fine." He said.

I don't know what's coming over me, but I want to kiss him, especially when he's near like this.

I immediately kissed him on the cheek and whispered in his ears,

"The food smells so good. If you keep treating me like this, I'm not going to want to leave." I didn't look at his expression but picked up the plate and ate.

"Let's watch the movie," I said between bites of the food.

I took a glance at him to find his cheeks red.

I held back a smile; he had better get used to this because I would definitely be very affectionate with him.

"Thank you." He said softly. I let out a small laugh.

"I'm pretty sure I should be thanking you. You've been nothing but nice to me, and I like you a lot. I feel like I'm being spoiled. I can't wait to see how spoiled I get treated when I reach boyfriend status." I said, shooting my shot. There was no way in hell I would let this opportunity slide away.

"You're serious about this, how?" he asked.

"Yes, very serious," I said, chuckling.

"Let's see what gave it away. Was it the kisses? The way I praise you? Or the way my eyes light up when I look at you? Or is it how you suddenly have made me feel something I have never felt before?" I asked him, giving him my full attention.

I wanted him to see how serious I was about this and seriously wanted to invest in this.

"Are you sure? I mean, I'm really nothing special," he said, and I rolled my eyes.

"Well, you're wrong about that, because you're something special. I am completely serious about what I said and I want to know a lot about you. I am serious about becoming your best friend and you becoming mine. I want to know about you and I promise you, you will learn things about me too." I said to him, smiling.

"Okay, we can give it a try," Ben said, and I felt overwhelmed with a burst of happiness.

Ben will need a lot of reassurance, which I wouldn't have a problem with.

"I didn't think you would be interested in knowing about me, especially my past," he said, and I shook my head, grabbing his hand.

"I would love too," I said with sincerity.

"Okay, but it's kind of a sad story," he said; I stayed quiet for a bit; the look on Ben's face showed me that whatever his past was, it was not for the weak or for someone who was just a passerby.

"It won't change how I feel about you now," I said; Ben stared at me briefly before he smiled softly.

"Okay." He said.

CH. 10 Letting someone in

C H.10 Letting someone in

(Ben POV)

"I'll tell you one day, I promise. If whatever happens to us ends up in a successful relationship, I'll tell you." I said.

"That's fine with me," Jesse said, smiling sweetly.

He kissed me again before turning his attention to the TV. I was going to have to get used to this.

I could feel my face getting heated, so I avoided it as I continued to eat while watching TV with him.

I don't know if anyone has ever felt what I felt, to wonder why someone was suddenly talking to them, showing them interest, and hanging out with them.

I wasn't the only one who had gone through this feeling; I'm sure some people could relate to what I was saying.

Right?

But I had no idea what to do; this was all new. It was sad and stupid to admit, but I didn't have that many people I considered friends. I never had any boyfriends or even flirted with a guy.

Yes.

I am a virgin, but I didn't mind being a virgin at all whatsoever; I mean, I wanted to do it with someone who was someone who fell for me, who I fell in love with as well.

Just because I was a virgin didn't mean I didn't have reasonable expectations for myself.

It didn't matter if I was a loner; I wanted someone to like me for me and be willing to be with me to get into a physical and emotional relationship.

Some people would call me a hopeless romantic, and I didn't care if I was seen as hopeless. I was allowed at least to think of what I wanted between my partner and me.

I glanced at him, and anyone could see that he was gorgeous.

He had the most beautiful skin I have ever seen, and his body was kept right. He was someone who made sure he took care of his body, and it showed.

I felt my face get heated as thoughts began to run through my head. I needed to stop thinking about this man's body; why was I behaving this way.

I tried to focus on the movie, but the thoughts would not go away. They had me thinking, of course. I know Jesse's a good kisser, obviously from him kissing me, but does that mean he's also good in-.

Okay, I need to stop.

I know for a fact that I would be the first guy he's ever dated, which means he does not have experience in gay sex, and I was a virgin, so what a great pair we were.

I smiled at the thought that if we ever got to that phase, it would be a new experience for both of us.

"What are you smiling about?" He asked me, and I looked up at him, not wanting him to know that I was actually having dirty thoughts about him.

I didn't want to freak him out, and there was no way I was bold enough to say what I was actually thinking.

"Just thinking it's going to be a journey for us, that's all," I said softly.

He rose a brow. "Well, I think of it as a nice adventure and I happen to like adventures. I know I will enjoy this one for sure." He said, going back to watching the TV.

My face was probably pink now. Jesse had a way with words that put you at ease.

When we were done eating, Jesse pulled me into his arms and cuddled me.

I laid my head against his chest. Resting my head against his chest felt terrific; it comforted me.

I was willing to open myself up to him, but of course, I was also scared because I had never done this before. I mean, just the thought of it was scary: letting someone in, letting them get to know you, your likes, your dislikes, what you're scared of, what bothers you, what you enjoy doing, and many more.

Also, you should let them learn about your past and why you're the way you are now.

That was scary, even though I had no friends. I knew I wasn't the only person who had felt like that.

I knew there were people out there who felt the way I felt.

Fingers started running through my hair, and my eyes began to flutter. Jesse started scratching my hair while running his fingers through it.

I found myself letting out a moan that honestly shocked me, but I just couldn't help it because it was something that I had never experienced. It was one of those best feelings, something you didn't want someone doing.

He kept doing it, not saying anything as I fell into bliss.

I could get used to it if he did this all the time. I would love to get this treatment in the morning and at night.

"You like that, don't you?" he asked me in a deep voice, and I whispered yes.

I really liked it.

"I can get used to this." I found myself saying before I could stop the words from coming out of my mouth.

"That's good because I want you too," he said, and I felt him lean in and kiss my neck.

I whimper at the touch; he lifted my head with his hand and brought my lips to his, kissing me.

I let my eyes close as he led the kiss, I kissed him back the best way I could, and a groan came from his mouth as he turned my body around, lifting me up and had me sitting on his lap.

I don't know how he did it or how I got into that position, but I was okay with it.

He stopped kissing me on the lips and lowered his lips on my neck, pressing kisses all over my neck, licking and sucking.

I moaned at the feeling, and he brought my body closer to his.

"I love the sound of your moans." He said while he brought his mouth towards my ear. He nibbled on my ear, which caused me to moan again.

Jesse tugged my head back towards him, bringing his lip back to mine, and I kissed him back with a force I didn't even know I had. I wanted him to feel how much I liked him, to see that I wanted him this way, too.

That I wanted us this way.

We both parted from our kiss moments later to catch our breaths. Jesse still had his eyes closed as he leaned his head against mine.

"You're amazing you know that?" He asked me, and I let out a small laugh.

"Not really," I said, causing Jesse's eyes to open up.

My breath hitched at how he looked, the seriousness in his eyes, and how intense his eye color looked.

"I'm going to show you how amazing you are to me. We're going to be dating, and there won't be a day that goes by that I don't show you how amazing you are," he said to me, and a smile made its way to my face.

"That's a promise." He said.

"Promises get broken sometimes," I whispered. Sadly, it was the truth. I've had promises made to me before that were sadly broken.

"Not this one, you'll see." He said, and I sure hoped he had proved me wrong.

After all, none of the books I've read said letting someone in would be easy.

(*Kassandra Speaks*)

Aww, I think Ben is all of us when we're getting into something new or even when we're getting into a relationship, and someone like Jesse comes along, who is good for us, but because of all the things we have gone through, because of the trust issues we have and the number of times we've gotten hurt, we're scared to let that person in.

Ben and Jesse are what they need from each other. Like Jesse said, this is an adventure, and of course, Jesse is starting to make Ben Feel. Their story is going to get amazing! Just wait, until next time, DOLLS

Give this chapter a VOTE, COMMENT & SHARE.

Xoxoxo

-Kassandra Vivu

CH. 11 Bye for now

C h. 11 Bye for now

(Jesse POV)

It eventually came when I had to say goodbye and goodnight to Ben. Well, for now, that is. I spent the whole day with Ben; I enjoyed it too, but now that I was standing in front of the front door to his condo, I stood there staring at him as I was getting ready to leave.

That's when I realized I didn't want to leave but would have to.

I had to get him to trust me, but for some reason, I wanted to stay longer; I wanted to spend the night, not sleeping together or having sex, just being with him. Something told me Ben wasn't the type of person to even sleep around or was able to trust someone easily.

Which was definitely something that I liked.

"Well, I guess this is a bye for now," I said lamely, receiving a smile from him.

He honestly had those types of smiles that anyone would want to be the cause of.

Again, I wish the day had been longer somehow.

"Did you get yourself a uber?" He asked me, and I nodded my head.

"Trying to kick me out already?" I said jokily, but his eyes widened with a tint of blush added to his cheeks.

"No, of course not. I was just making sure you had a ride, that's all. Honestly, I enjoyed the day we had," he finished shyly.

"That's great, I hope you never get sick and tired of me. You're stuck with me. I should get going, the uber is here." I said.

"Do you want me to walk you out?" He asked me, and I shook my head, smiling.

"If you walk me out, I'm going to want you to get in the cab with me, so it's better if you just stay here," I said, noticing his red face.

"Okay, well, bye for now then," he said awkwardly. I held back a smile, not wanting to overly tease him.

"Trust me, when I head back to the hotel I am going to face time you. It'll feel like I never left in the first place." I said to him with a goofy smile.

I quickly gave him a peck on his lips before pulling back.

"I'll talk to you later," I said, opening his front door and exiting.

Why was that the hardest thing for me to do? Especially towards someone I just met?

I walked out of the building and got in the Uber that was waiting for me.

The Uber driver's eyes widened, probably from realizing who I was. Of course, he asked for an autograph. I didn't mind, signed it, and spoke to him during the drive.

I signed some things for him and also took a picture with him. During the drive, I asked the Uber driver about the area, stuff he recommended for fun, and sights to see. I noted everything we discussed and was brainstorming ideas for Ben and me on the next date.

I asked the Uber driver if he wanted to be my driver while I was in town, as I liked his personality. He immediately accepted and gave me his card.

He dropped me off in front of the hotel, and I waved goodbye to him as I entered the building.

As soon as I got in, I texted my agent, Amber, letting her know I needed to talk to her as quickly as possible.

When I got to my suite, Amber was already calling me.

Not only was Amber my agent, but she was also my best friend and a person I could trust with anything. I needed to tell her about what had already happened and how I was interested in someone. Although I know I wouldn't tell her everything now, giving some details is safe.

"What's up? How is everything there? I'll be there in a couple of days," she said as I approached the hotel living room.

"Amber, hear me out, okay? I met someone, and I like that person. I am also considering dating that person, and as my agent, I need you to be prepared to back me up no matter what and have everything already in the powerhouse so no one can twist any stories about the person that I am interested in dating." I said to her, serious about what I was talking about.

People like to spread false narratives, and I didn't want that happening about Ben and me.

"Woah, Woah, Woah. You sound extremely serious about this. I am willing to always back you up, but I think it's funny how you're over there for work, the interview, and other things, but somehow you found someone you like. It's funny as you didn't even want to go there in the first place," she laughed.

"Actually, let me Facetime you right now. I need to know how serious you're about this," she said.

I answered her Facetime call and continued the conversation.

"Why would you need to Facetime me to see if I'm serious?" I asked curiously.

"Your facial expressions tell me if you're joking, lying, or serious. So who is this person, and what is she like?" she asked me, with a curious look on her face.

"He's the journalist that interviewed me," I said, her mouth dropping open as she looked at me.

She closed her mouth and shrugged.

"Okay, well, that's surprising, but it's cool. So you like him?" Amber asked me, and I nodded my head. Appreciating that she wasn't grilling me with many questions, especially ones that I could not answer right now.

"Yeah, I'm serious. I don't know why I feel this way but I want to go through with this." I said.

I want to go through my feelings for Ben right now.

"Well, I'm not going to sugarcoat this for you, but it will be tough going through this, first being a football player and second being a celebrity." She said. I nodded, agreeing with Amber. It was true. This is going to take a lot of work.

"Yeah, I know but it's 2019 and I don't care what anyone has to say. If the football players on the football team feel a certain way I'll settle it down, I'm still a great player and I won't be disrespected because of who I decide to be in a relationship with." I said.

Amber smiled at me.

"That's my boy. I'm proud. I would like to meet him when I get there. You really seem serious about someone you just met. He must be really special," she said with a raised brow.

"I'm going to Facetime him now. I'll talk to you tomorrow." I started to say but immediately stopped when I noticed Amber's appearance.

She was dressed up and glammed up; she was up to something or going somewhere. She didn't even think to tell me; she just sat there listening to me talk about things I had going on. What about her?

"Why are you wearing that dress? Where are you going?" I asked her, and her eyes widened.

"Bye, lover boy! I'm hanging up now," she said, ending the Facetime call. I stared at the dark screen of my phone, shocked that she did not even let out a small detail about why she was all dressed up the way she was. I was going to ask her many questions when I talked to her next time.

I FaceTimed Ben, unable to hold back my smile on how quickly he answered my Facetime call.

As soon as I saw his face, my smile widened even more.

"Well, Hello Beautiful," I said.

(*Kassandra Speaks*)

Aww, how cute is Jesse? If he wants something or someone, Jesse is the type of guy who will fight to get that person or something no matter what, which is what he is doing right now.

But do you all think Jesse is ready?

Do you all think Ben is ready?

Of course, love is love, but remember, we live in a world where everyone is not very accepting.

Football players especially can have it hard.

Well, this is another journey we will be joining.

Give this chapter a

VOTE, COMMENT & SHARE!

I'll see you all in the next update.

Xoxoxox

-Kassandra Vivu

CH. 12 He called me beautiful

CH. 12 He called me Beautiful

(Ben POV)

Did he just call me beautiful?

His smile confirmed that he did. I felt my face getting heated, and indeed, by the way his smile widened, my face was most likely red by now.

Now, receiving a compliment about my looks was something I had never received. I didn't think I was good-looking myself. I was somewhat decent-looking, and I was happy with my looks.

It's just that having someone else give you compliments was on another level.

Why? Because someone else thought you were attractive and told you that you were.

It was the first time someone had ever called me beautiful.

It was a compliment I didn't think I would ever get, especially being a male.

Honestly, It felt nice, but it also made me nervous.

I was nervous because I was feeling things I had never felt before; I was experiencing things I never thought I would experience. This frightened me, but it also made me happy.

"Do you think I'm beautiful?" I asked, raising a brow, and he threw his head back, laughing.

"It's more like I know you're. So you're getting ready for bed?" Jesse asked me.

My eyes widened, and I noticed that Jesse was blushing himself.

I held back a smile, enjoying how we were flirting.

I was in my bed, under the covers, and all tucked in.

"Yes," I answered him.

"You look cute, I told my agent and close friend about you already." He said, causing my eyes to widen.

He had already spoken about me to someone. I felt fuzzy at the thought that this person was serious about starting something with me.

"Oh really? How did that go? I must say you're surprising me each moment you get, I didn't think you would tell someone already." I said softly, and this time, he raised a brow.

He got himself into his bed and spoke. "Really? Well, I told you I was serious about being with you, and I meant that. Anyways, it was my agent, who is also a very close friend of mine, that I told, and I trust her, so have no fear—you won't be posted all over the tabloids." He said jokily, but my eyes widen.

"Well, we would need to know more about each other before letting people know that we're together when we get together. Also, I would appreciate it if we didn't let other people know for a while. I'm fine with your close friends who you know and trust and your family members who you know and trust, but you're basically a celebrity, and I've seen how it gets when regular people date celebrities and it's crazy. You and I know we're together, your close friends and family will know too. No one else should matter to us." I said nervously.

Jesse smiled softly.

"Yeah, I know what you mean. When we're ready to let the rest of the outside people in our lives know about the relationship we're going to have, then we will," he said.

I breathed a breath of relief I didn't know I was holding.

"You know, I miss your presence already," he said, causing me to smile.

"You just saw me and you miss me already? I'm actually quite touched. That's honestly pretty nice." I said, teasing him, which had him chuckling.

"Well, yeah, I mean, it's not every day you find someone that you like, are able to click with, and want to be in your life, you know. I'm glad I came across that, and I am not letting it go at all," he said.

"That's good, so what made you get into football?" I asked him to change the topic. I was okay with putting our emotions out there, but I also decided to go through with this and wanted to get to know him more.

"Well, I've been playing football all my life; like I said before I played many sports. My dad also played football. He's a pretty cool laid back dude and I can't wait to introduce you to him. He's very accepting by the way, which most people wouldn't assume for some reason when it comes to my dad. He looks scary, big, tall and buff but dude is actually a teddy bear who has love for everyone. Those are my mother words by the way. Now, my mom, she's actually a nerd. I'm talking about a huge nerd, she's in love with books, history, literature, you name it and I love hearing the story of how her and my dad met. I'm sure they will tell you it as soon as they meet you." He said; my heart tightened at how happy he got talking about his parents.

"My sister is a goofball, and to be quite honest, I think you will like her also. My friend Amber, who's also my agent and manager, is a really good person. I have many good people in my life. I can't wait for you and me to know each other really well so we can get towards that point where I can introduce you to them." He said, and I slowly nodded.

"I wish there was someone I could introduce you to but I don't really have anyone. I never bothered making friends, I mean I have co-workers of course who always compliment my work and invite me to get food with them or drinks, but I always decline saying I'm busy. My boss also tries to be my friend, even though I've been giving him the vibe that I don't need any friends he never stops trying. He's a good guy, I'm just socially awkward sometimes. I did have some people I was close with when I was younger, a group of girls but I lost touch with them." I said, letting out a soft laugh to soften my words.

His face was grave when he said the following words.

"Well, you have me now. I also think that you'll be able to make decent friends. It's just harder for some people than others, but you will get to that point," Jesse said with an understanding tone.

"It's hard, I'm not an easy person to understand, and I am not trying to say I'm complicated, but I feel like that's the vibe I've given, and I don't know how to fix that," I said.

"Lucky you, I do puzzles daily with my mom and I especially loved the complicated ones." He said, causing my heart to tighten.

"You sure good at making people catch feelings," I said, causing a cocky smile to appear on Jesse's face.

"I want you to catch feelings as much as I am catching feelings. You are what matters right now," Jesse said.

Jesse has no idea that he is already making me feel many things I have not felt in my whole life, and I was going to allow myself to have those feelings. I was going to allow myself to finally fall for someone.

(*Kassandra Speaks*)

I like how Ben and Jesse's relationship is going. I like their vibe together.

Anyway, give this chapter a

VOTE & Comment!!

The next chapter is interesting!!

Xoxoxo

-Kassandra Vivu

Ch. 13 Don't let it get to you

C H. 13 Don't let it get to you

(Ben POV)

I was going towards the break room when I heard my name being mentioned.

I stood next to the wall, listening to what was being said. Of course, my co-workers were talking about me.

"Do you think he thinks he's better than us?" a voice that I recognized as Derrick.

"We always invite him to have drinks with us, and he turns us down. He's always getting ahead of his work, making it seem like we're slacking when we're all going at a normal pace," Lucas, another co-worker, said.

A woman's voice spoke.

"You two need to cut it. So what if he doesn't want to hang out with you both, and so what if he's always more invested in work? It's his life, and some people don't care for groupies or wanting to hang out; some people just want to work and go home to be alone after a long day of work or some people just don't want to hang out with their co workers," The woman voice said.

It was another co-worker named Lilian.

She was one of those co-workers who always spoke to me and have always been friendly with me.

"Yeah right, that dude has no friends and is a loner with a lame personality," Derrick said.

"Well because of his lame personality, he got to have an interview with Jesse Hutcherman and you didn't get picked for that. He's good at his job and he doesn't do anything to bother you. Just stop taking it to heart and let it go, it's not like he's ever done anything to you." Lilian said.

A laugh came. "Woah Lilian guess you have a crush on Ben huh?" Lucas said.

"No, I like him. He's a good guy. I am just being the adult I am who doesn't have a child mindset like you two. What the hell are you? Elementary kids? Apparently, talking behind a fellow employee's back like that." Lilian's voice raised, and my eyes widened now that their tone was getting louder.

This would not be good if a full-blast argument ended up happening.

"We didn't say anything but the truth," Derrick said, and I heard Lilian laugh.

"We didn't say anything but the truth." She mimicked Derrick.

"This is why you guys aren't doing well; look how you both behave," she said.

I took that time to walk into the break room.

The room fell quiet. From outside the break room, I thought it would be just Lilian, Derrick, and Lucas. My eyes widened when I realized that 10 people were in the break room, but only Lilian stood up for me.

Derrick and Lucas tried to play it off like they weren't talking about me.

"Hey, Ben," Derrick said, and I raised a brow.

"Talking shit behind my back but can't say it to my face? Save your Hi." I said, Lilian, and let out a laugh.

I walked to the fridge to get my lunch.

I turned towards Lilian.

"Thanks for having my back," I said, giving her a small smile.

"No problem; I just can't be fake like the others," she said, giving me a small smile.

I nodded and gave a farewell wave as I left the break room.

I heard Lilian's laugh, knowing she was laughing at Lucas and Derrick.

I should talk to her more. She's been nothing but pleasant to me.

I walked towards my desk and was about to start my lunch. I heard my boss call my name from his office.

I walked towards his office, going in and closing the door behind me.

My boss was beaming.

"I went over the interview, Ben. It was great, kiddo! I knew my star jounalist could do it. I liked it, and I sent it forward. Everyone liked it also. Hey, what's wrong?" he asked me.

I raised a brow, wondering why he was asking me such a question.

"You seem upset?" He asked.

My eyes widened; I could never understand how this man could know how I was feeling.

I was good at hiding my emotions, and ever since this man hired me for an internship and then leveled me up to different positions within the company, he's always been able to tell my moods no matter how good my poker face was.

"Who's bothering you?" He asked me. I shook my head.

"It's nothing serious to worry yourself about," I said.

He shook his head, not letting me brush it off.

"No, Ben. I like you, kid. I see you as a son. Hell, I don't even have a son, and me seeing you as a son means a lot. Don't let them get to you, and if they're bothering you, do something great that will make them feel ashamed that they ever thought to bother you." I nodded my head, and he let out a sigh.

I did want to avoid getting into this more. I felt relieved when my boss changed the topic.

"So, how was meeting Jesse Hutcherman?" he asked, and when his name was mentioned, my face got heated.

I look at the boss and find his mouth dropped open.

Alarm ran through my body, scared of what he might think. I knew from the facial expression I gave out that he most likely figured out by my reaction that I was gay.

"Well, Damn. I didn't see that coming. So did you enjoy the meeting or what?" He asked.

My eyes widened. My boss shrugged his shoulder, showing me that he didn't mind.

I nodded my head.

"Yeah, it went well. He's a cool person," I said, causing my boss's eyes to widen.

"Oooooh, so you like him like him." He said, giving me a small smile.

I don't know my facial expression, but he chuckled loudly.

"I'm liking these facial expressions, usually someone else would have said. That this couldn't happen, but I'm all for it. Honestly, kid, I want you happy and I want you interacting with people who want you in their lives. So what's that thing that these kids call it nowadays. When you approve of people getting to know each other or dating. Oh yeah, I ship it." He said, chuckling.

I lightly facepalmed myself at my boss, trying to be in touch with this year's slang terms.

"Well, I guess you can call me a matchmaker since I'm the reason you two met. I guess I should change professions," he said, rubbing his chin.

Which got a small laugh from me. He smiled softly at me.

"Thanks, Steve, for the matchmaking," I said shyly.

"Alright, son, I'm going to let you go back to your lunch. You can extend it by the way, until you're actually finished eating because I know I cut it short with me talking to you and all." He said.

I thanked him and left his office.

Walking back to my desk, I noticed Lilian sitting on her seat eating.

She probably couldn't take being in the break room anymore.

I called out to her; Lilian stared at me with a shocked expression.

Even though I was shocked by what I had just done, I didn't back down.

"Would you like to have lunch with me?" I asked, and she smiled, grabbing her food quickly and coming my way.

"You bet ya." She said, laughing.

I don't know why, but meeting Jesse has made me feel many things.

I was starting to like it.

(*Kassandra Speaks*)

Oh, so you like like him. Lol, oh my gosh, anyways, there's this thing that's been going on where people are repeating the same word twice to get their thoughts across, and I thought it was silly at first, but then I got a kick out of it.

Ben is starting to change slightly, and he says it's because of meeting Jesse; hmm, do you all agree?

I love how Lilian stood up for Ben. We all know things like that happen everywhere, and it does not matter who stands up for you as long as someone stands up for you in your absence.

Give this chapter a VOTE, COMMENT & SHARE. See you all in the next update!!!!!!!!!!!

XOXOXO

-Kassandra Vivu

CH. 14 Baby I got you

CH.14 Baby, I got you.

(Jesse POV)

I was in the hotel room, making dinner. Why, you ask? Because Ben is coming over, we'll spend the night eating, talking, and watching movies. It would be a good night, and I look forward to it.

I couldn't wait for Ben to come over so we could talk and for him to tell me about his day.

Even though I saw him yesterday, I wasn't joking when I said I missed his presence.

I placed some food on the table and smiled at the setup.

I was okay with getting used to or doing this all the time.

I had our movie options picked out already, and dessert was in the oven.

Shit, maybe I should play some music also?

I went to my laptop, connected the speakers, and played Italian music.

I went to pull the dessert out of the oven when a knock came from the door.

I yelled, saying I was coming, putting the red velvet cake on the kitchen counter, and headed towards the front door.

I looked through the peephole and couldn't stop smiling as I saw Ben standing on the other side.

"Hello, Beautiful," I said, opening the door and getting a small chuckle from Ben.

I moved aside to let him in, checking him out as he walked in.

Does he know that he looks good?

Does he know that he's a very handsome man? I should let him know that.

I closed the door and pulled Ben into my arms, resting my head on his shoulder.

"You look very handsome, and Mmm, you smell good too," I said, kissing his cheek.

He pulled out of my arms and turned to face me; a hint of blush was seen on his cheek.

"Do I?" He asked, and I nodded my head.

"Yes, baby you do," I said, noticing his face getting redder.

He looked around, smiling.

"Music playing, candle lights, and food on the table that smells really good. Wow, you went all out, I see." He said softly, looking shyly around, but I could tell by the look on his face that he was delighted.

"Of course I did. I wanted to do this for you today. Now have a seat," I said, taking Ben's hand and bringing him to a chair. I pulled it out for him, and he sat down.

I sat in front of him, smiling.

"Let's start eating and talking," I said, Ben chuckled with an amused look.

"Okay," he said, taking a bite of the food. I let him take the first bite because I wanted to know his thoughts. I watched as his eyes widened.

"This is really good." He said, causing me to smile.

Feeling happy with my hard work.

"Good, I'm glad you like it. Now, how was your day?" I asked him, taking a bite of my food, too.

He talked about his day, explaining what happened earlier, with co-workers talking behind his back in the break room, and that only one co-worker stood up for him.

I shook my head.

"Those assholes are lowkey jealous. don't let them get to you and I'm glad that someone spoke against them. I can tell that you take your job very seriousily, it's something that you've worked hard on and seem to continue to work hard on. That is definitely amazing and something to be proud of, of course, you're going to have haters and people trying to bring you down. It's okay, it's something that's sadly common in every field." I said truthfully.

"And whenever you have a bad day, I'll be here to uplift you. You don't have to go through any of that alone, not anymore," I said, looking at him.

It was true.

I want to be that type of person for him.

Whenever we get into our relationship, I want to be the person where he feels like he can talk about anything his heart desires.

Ben seemed to be taking my words in as I stared at him. He looked like he was debating what to say.

"You really mean that?" He asked me, a soft look coming across his face.

I nodded my head.

"Of course I do, I'm not going anywhere. I know it's hard to believe that, at this moment but it's true. I am not going anywhere and I will prove that to you in every way I can." I said, taking another bite of my food and giving him a smirk.

I wanted to be a part of Ben's life; I know we just met, but I feel we should be together and enjoy being together.

"You're my reward, It would be an honor to have you as mine," I said. I noticed his face instantly getting red.

"You're so cute. I love making you blush. I'm sorry I couldn't help it," I said, laughing, knowing my mom would go crazy over Ben and fuss over how cute he was. I would have never thought I would be awestruck by someone like this.

"What did you do all day?" He asked me.

"I spoke to my parents, my sister, and Amber. I also watched some of my highlights and planned our dinner," I said, smiling.

"Can you show me some of your highlights sometimes?" He said, taking me off guard; I didn't think he would be interested.

"Of course, I'll show my baby my highlights anytime. Heck, maybe you might even get into watching me play football." I said, teasing him a little.

I saw him roll his eyes, smiling.

The way the word baby rolled off my tongue when it came to speaking to him was something that I found myself enjoying.

"I mean, I might have to get into it, considering it's what you do for a living. You play football; I don't mind supporting you by watching or going to your games," Ben said, and I felt my face get heated at the thought of having him on the stand while I was on the field playing.

"Is that okay?" He asked, analyzing my face. I nodded my head. Thrilled that he brought that up.

"That's really great. I would really like that," I said, a broad smile on Ben's face.

"Really?" He asked.

"Yeah, I would also love to see you wear one of my jerseys and have my jersey number written with face paint or marker on your cheeks," I said, smiling. I was already picturing it and loving every moment.

"Well, if you're fine with that I can do it." He said.

"Yeah, it would be awesome," I said, unable to hide my smile.

Ben laughed shyly as he stared at me.

For some reason, that laugh brought a flutter to my body.

I cleared my throat.

"Come here," I said to Ben; he raised a brow. A confused look appeared on his face.

"Please," I said; Ben pushed back his seat, got up, and walked towards me.

I pushed my seat back also.

I watched as he came and stood next to me.

I pulled his body towards me and made him sit on my lap facing me.

A bold move for both of us, but for some reason. I had the urge to want Ben closer to me.

His eyes widened at the position we were in.

"I just wanted to be closer to you," I said, wrapping my arms around him.

"You smell so good," I said, putting my nose to his neck and inhaling his scent.

I licked his neck.

"You taste good too," I said.

I felt a shudder run through Ben's body as he sat on my lap.

Ben's fingers made their way into my hair, where he ran his fingers up and down my head.

While he was doing so, my lips were still against his neck, pressing kisses, licking and sucking on it.

The noises he was letting out had me nibbling his neck even more.

"Jesse." He moaned, causing me to grab his hips and pull him closer.

I could not hide what I felt for Ben right now. I was hard as a rock and knew he would immediately feel it.

He gasped when he noticed the hardness, and I held him there, wanting him to feel how hard I was.

I brought my mouth towards his ear, nibbling on his earlobe.

"You see what you do to me baby," I whispered in his ear.

"Mmm," Ben said, leaned closer, and got lost in the touching and nibbling I was doing.

I felt him start to move his hips back and forth, which took me off guard.

He was dry-humping me, Ben was dry-humping, and damn sure I held on to his hips while he was doing it. I moved my head to stare at him; his eyes were closed, and he looked like he was letting himself loose.

I let out a groan.

"Fuck, Baby, don't stop," I said, feeling myself get harder; Ben was positioned precisely on top of my cock; I knew he felt me get harder, and the way he moaned as he tilted his head to the side confirmed that.

I watched as he let noises out, noises that had me never wanting them to end. I watched his face as he rode me; I watched him move his hips, his body on my hard-on.

I grabbed his head and slammed my lips on his.

Ben never stopped his riding. I moaned through our kiss, loving every moment of this.

Fuck, he doesn't know how hot he is.

I rolled my tongue against his lips, asking for entrance; Ben allowed it as we both twirled our tongues together, deepening the kiss.

A few minutes passed from our make-out session, and we finally stopped to get air.

"Fuck, you're so hot," I said; Ben's eyes were in a daze as he leaned his forehead against mine.

"You're hard." He said. I opened my eyes to look at him.

"Of course I would get hard for you, baby. Did you think I wouldn't?" I asked, but he didn't have to answer because the look on his face gave me the answer.

I gave him a peck.

"I'll always get hard when it comes to you and only you," I said, saying my last words softly.

His eyes widen.

"I'm hard also." He whispered, and I smiled.

"Good," I said, feeling happy that he was; it proved that his body wanted me.

We stayed quiet for a few minutes, just enjoying each other's company, as we were in each other's arms until Ben spoke.

"I like you, I like you a lot." He said, and I smiled.

"I like you too," I said, smiling.

(*Kassandra Speaks*)

Give this chapter a VOTE & COMMENT!

See you all in the next CHAPTER.

Xoxoxo

-Kassandra Vivu

CH. 15 We're Dating

C H. 15 We're Dating.

(Ben POV)

I was sitting behind my desk doing work when I felt someone's eyes on me. I planned to avoid it, but I dared myself to look up.

When I looked up, I made eye contact with Derrick; he looked taken off guard that I actually made eye contact with him.

I lowered my head and returned to work, not overthinking, mainly because I didn't care.

He was talking crap about me behind my back the other day with Lucas anyway.

All these Journalists here made it seem like I didn't work my ass off to get here where I was; I didn't get anything handed to me at all whatsoever.

I wasn't the type to drag things out, so I let it go after talking to Jesse about it yesterday.

People are going to hate you regarding anything sometimes. They will find something they don't like about you and might even try to make you feel bad about it.

I won't feel wrong about me doing my job, about me doing something that I can actually do.

It wasn't my fault they weren't working as hard as me. They needed to be working on improving themselves.

Everything I do is for myself; everything I work on is for myself. I do everything for me.

As I was working, I thought about what happened last night and couldn't stop smiling.

My face heated, recalling last night's memories and how Jesse had kissed and made me feel.

This was something that I wasn't used to, but I definitely didn't mind it.

I like having Jesse in my life, and I look forward to seeing him as much as possible.

The fact that he prepared dinner for us yesterday and the meal he made was delicious.

"Woah, is that a smile." I looked up to find Lilian holding two cups of coffee.

She smiled and placed coffee in front of me.

Oh, I so needed this coffee.

I smiled back at her, showing my appreciation for her bringing me coffee.

"Thank you. I really needed this," I said. Lilian laughed, nodding her head in agreement.

"Yeah, I know what you mean; it's nice to see a smile on your face." She said, and my smile widened.

"Something good must have happened, huh?" I nodded, and she smiled.

"Good, I'm glad. What are you working on?" Lilianshe asked me as I sipped my coffee before speaking.

"I'm writing an article about the elections and the movements that are going on," I said, an interested look appeared on her face.

"That is driving me crazy; the whole politics thing is driving me mad," she said, I nodded, agreeing with her. It has been a messy election time, indeed.

She took a sip of her coffee, turned around, glanced at something, and then turned back to look at me.

Bringing a chair to sit next to me, she lowered her head on her hand and spoke.

"Um, I think Derrick has been stealing looks at you," Lilian said.

"I noticed that he was looking at me earlier, but I have no idea why. I'm paying him no attention, though," I said, humming as Lilian tapped her fingers on the desk.

"I'm literally trying my best not to ask him what he's looking at. I'm trying to be nice today," Lilian said, causing me to laugh.

"Is that so?" I asked; a smirk appeared as she rolled her eyes.

"Yeah, something about my horoscope said to be nice to the people who don't deserve it today and something good will be coming soon. So, I'm going to be nice and not snap at Derrick, even though I'm sure you can feel his stare right now as much as I can." She said, and I smiled.

"Yeah, I can." I said

She ran her fingers through her hair.

"I would say maybe he has a crush on you, but I'm not a hundred percent sure yet, I mean if he does. He has a weird way of showing it, I mean, what are we in grade school?" She said, taking me off guard.

Did she say a crush?

No way. I doubt that he does, and she was right that if he did, it would be a weird way of showing it.

"I'm not sure it's a crush, I think he just hates me," I said.

"You've literally done nothing to anyone at all what so ever, all you've done is your work. Honestly, you come to work, work hard and do what you got to do, then you leave. There's nothing wrong with that." She said, and it was true. That there was nothing wrong with that.

"Thanks for understanding that," I said.

"Don't mind them; people get mad over everything now," Lilian said in a low tone.

"I'm glad to see you at least opening up a little bit; it's nice having you talk to me," she said; her voice sounded overly genuine, so I looked up at her to make eye contact.

"Yeah, it's nice. Sorry. It's just that I've gone through a lot. I'm not really that much of an open person, and it's really hard for me to trust people. I'm glad that you've always kept trying to talk to me and never stopped being nice to me," I said honestly. Lilian smiled, a dimple appearing on each cheek.

"Of course, I totally understand. Don't worry. People go through many things that shape their lives to what they are today. I've also gone through things that have changed my character. There's nothing to apologize for, Ben." She said, and I honestly felt at that moment that Lilian would be a very good friend of mine.

I had a good day today. I finished my article and showed it to my boss, who approved and praised my work.

I was heading to my condo.

I instantly smiled when I saw Jesse standing next to my door, who looked up at the sound of footsteps.

He smiled.

"Well, hello there, handsome. I thought I would come over and surprise you," he said.

"I'm surprised. Come in." I said, unlocking my door and letting him in.

I ensured Jesse was entirely inside the condo before I closed and locked the door.

I turned to face him, finding him staring at me with a soft smile.

"Is it weird to say that I miss you." He said, causing my heart to leap.

"No, It's not," I said in a whisper.

He walked towards me and gave me a peck.

He lowered his head on my neck and breathed in my scent.

"Good, because I miss my baby." He said, nibbling on my neck; he licked and sucked the same area, causing me to let out a small whimper at the feeling I felt.

He pulled away and kissed my forehead.

"Come on, let's sit on the couch, and you can tell me about your day," he said; Jesse told me yesterday that it would be a habit for him to ask me how my day is.

"You want to know about my day?" I asked with a shy smile. Jesse nodded.

"I always want to hear about your day." He said.

"Are we dating?" I asked him, causing his eyes to widen.

"Yes, do you want us to be dating?" Jesse asked me.

"Yes." I found myself saying.

"That's Good because we are definitely dating each other," he said.

"Good, I'm glad we're here," I said, lightly pushing him to sit on the couch. I got on the sofa but decided to lie, placing my head on his lap.

I brought Jesse's hand to my mouth and kissed it.

I kissed it softly, wanting to do a few things I'd seen on TV and calling him cute names, such as baby and honey.

"Okay, honey. This is how my day went." I said, deciding to go with honey.

(*Kassandra Speaks*)

I love how Lilian is a really laid-back person and is actually trying to be Ben's friend; I also like how Ben has been improving and is actually willing to let some people in; he still has a long journey to go through, of course, and you will see that in a couple of chapters but it's nice to see that he's trying. You know. I love how Jesse is with Ben and doesn't hide his feelings. What do you all think was Derrick's Problem? Why do you all think he was staring at Ben?

Give this chapter a VOTE & COMMENT

.

See you all in the next update.

Xoxoxo

-Kassandra Vivu

CH. 16 Yes, Open up

Ch. 16 Yes, Open up

(Jesse POV)

I didn't realize that meeting someone and watching them start to feel comfortable and open up to me bit by bit would make me feel all these happy emotions.

It's a beautiful feeling.

I was getting that from Ben; I immediately melted when he kissed my lips.

I felt myself getting hot; it was such a sweet gesture to me, and I was happy that I was able to experience it.

I was happy when he did that.

He explained his day to me, also mentioning that guy named Derrick.

He told me how Lilian said that Derrick kept staring at him and that he felt Derrick's stares but decided to avoid them.

My guard immediately went up. From the moment Ben first mentioned Derrick and that other prick, I knew I wouldn't like either.

That Derrick guy has been staring at Ben in a way that Ben could actually feel his staring didn't settle well with me.

"Well, if he gives you problems I'll have to do something about it because I am not letting anyone mess with you," I said, meaning the words that left my mouth.

There is no way I would let people mess with my Ben.

He gave me a soft smile that made me feel a certain way. It was like I had just received a gift I was looking forward to.

I placed a kiss on his head.

"I'm serious, okay baby, I won't tolerate anyone thinking that they could mess around with you and I am so glad, that Lilian and you, are becoming friends," I said, as he let out a small laugh.

"So you're the overprotective type of person, huh? And yes, I actually appreciated that she never gave up on getting us to become friends. She's a nice and cool person; I am just a person who has trouble opening up to people, that's all." Ben said.

I pulled my lips away from his forehead to look at him, and he looked shyly away.

"It's fine baby, you can take your time with letting anyone in. Including me. Everyone is different, everyone is allowed to let who they want in their lives and who they don't want in their lives. There's nothing wrong with that okay and don't you feel like it is. I am honestly glad you're opening up more though. I honestly really like it and I am honored to have you open up to me and I will never take it for granted." I said to him.

"Is that so?" He asked me, and I nodded my head.

"Of course baby. When I say something to you. I mean it, all of it." I said.

Ben stared at me, not saying anything until a shy smile appeared.

"How was your day?" He asked me, and I shrugged my shoulders.

"It was a pretty normal day, I am on a break here so I barely have anything to do. I did expand my time here and I am so glad I did, I like being around you. By the way Amber said she can't wait to meet you but of course I won't let her meet you until you're ready to meet her. She's one of my best friends and she's a sweetheart but, I want you to be comfortable around the important people in my lives and if you're not ready to meet certain people yet. Then I can simply just wait until you're ready to." I said, watching his reaction.

Ben nodded and stayed quiet for a few minutes before he spoke again.

"I understand, I mean I wouldn't mind meeting her at all, but I might be quiet around her at first. As I said, I am trying and I am willing to try but of course, things just don't change overnight so I am still the same shy Ben, just trying to get out of the shell that's all, it's just taking me a while that's all." He said. I understood what he meant, which was fine with me.

"Everyone has their own finish line, it doesn't matter how long it takes you to reach it, it doesn't matter if you take a couple of breaks before you reach it. You just have to reach it, never give up on reaching it and going across it. You owe it to yourself. It's fine dealing with it the way you feel fit, it's fine taking your time for yourself because that line isn't going anywhere. It's your line and it's going to be there for you, forever." I said.

Ben stared at me with wide eyes, then started laughing, which confused me but amused me simultaneously.

"You have a way with words you know?" He asked me.

"Do I?" I asked in an amused tone.

"Yes, I like it. It's like you're my little philosopher." Ben said.

"I like being yours," I said in a low voice.

"Is that so?" He asked me, and I smiled at him.

"Yes, can I kiss you?" I asked him, I wanted to kiss him, but I wanted to ask for his permission.

"You don't have to ask," he said shyly, and I raised my hand towards the back of his head so I could bring his head towards me and place my lips on his lips.

I felt Ben move; he positioned himself to sit on my lap. I moaned against his lips, loving that this was the second time he had done this.

He is so cute.

I instantly took control of the kiss, showing him how much I've missed being around him today.

I found myself getting hard every single time I kissed Ben; I was like a teenager, liking someone for the first time. I was slightly annoyed with it, not being able to control my hard-on around him, but I simply couldn't help it as well.

I moved my lips away from his mouth, and Ben made a sad noise that tugged at my heart. He's really freaking cute.

I chuckled as I got ready to move him from my lap, but the following words that came out of Ben's mouth made me instantly stop, wanting nothing more than to just continue having my way with him.

"Please don't stop," Ben said.

(*Kassandra Speaks*)

Are you in love with these two relationships? Aren't they cute? What should their ship names be?

Give this chapter a VOTE & COMMENT

XOXO

-Kassandra Vivu

CH. 17 He said to ride it

C H. 17 He said to ride it

(Ben Pov)

It took me off guard that those words that came from me.

I asked him not to stop. I just told Jesse not to stop. This surprised me in many ways. I did not think I would ever voice something like that out loud. On the other, I was so in the mood that I wanted more of him touching me.

"You can ride it like last time." He said in a deep voice that caused my eyes to widen.

I could feel my face turning red.

I knew what he was referring to, but for some reason, I was even more nervous about being put on the spot and reminded of how I was last time with him.

"Don't be nervous, baby. It's yours," he said; Jesse raised my head to make direct eye contact.

"You can take control if you like." He said.

I nodded slowly, unsure what to do with the new role he had given me.

I was in control. Jesse and I responded as if we couldn't keep our hands off each other. Was this normal?

I leaned my face against his neck and did what I had done before; I moved my body on him and heard the noises coming from Jesse, which gave me the courage to continue to do more.

A moan suddenly came out of his mouth, causing my face to get hotter.

"Fuck." He said when I quickened my pace.

"Baby." He said, tugging on my shirt. I stopped what I was doing, looked down at his face, and found his whole face red and his eyes dazed.

"Just let me take off my pants. You can take yours off, too, if you want. I just want to feel you better," he said. I nodded my head nervously, knowing that if we were just in our underwear, the fabric would be much thinner than our pants, and we would be able to feel each other even more.

I watched as he stood up and took off his pants.

I did the same, letting my pants drop to the floor.

My eyes didn't waver from Jesse's lower region; there was a massive tent in front of me, and it stood up, alerted.

He sat back on the couch, and I looked up to find him staring at me with a look that caused me to whimper.

"Come back here," he said in the same deep voice from earlier, but this time, just what he said caused shivers to run down my body.

I walked towards him and spread my legs to sit on him; he looked at me and pulled my face towards his for a kiss, which I happily gave, feeling the warmth of his lips press against mine.

I let him take control of the kiss and went back to what I was doing before.

He was right; it was better without the pants on, and for some reason, I voiced that.

Jesse let out a groan after I did and continued to kiss me.

I was getting bolder with my words and wasn't holding back.

I wanted him to know how much he made me feel, that he made me feel things that I didn't feel before, and I voiced those things out loud as I rode him more.

I watched as Jesse continued to moan, resting his head on the couch as he stared at me with a dazed expression.

His look of satisfaction boosted me even more, the fact that I was making him feel this way.

The fact that I was dry-riding Jesse Hutcherman, the fucking football player.

The fact that he was mine, My boyfriend, and he wanted me, only me.

It turned me on even more; it made me even hornier.

I let out a loud moan when he grabbed my hips and moved under me.

"You're so fucking beautiful." He said as he buried his head on my neck, kissing and sucking on it.

I loved it when he did that; it drove me crazy and excited me.

It made me feel like I was highly sexy even though I didn't feel like it; I liked it when he said and did things like what he just did.

It helped give me confidence, and I wanted him to know; I played with Jesse's hair as he sucked on my neck.

Being bold and telling him how impressed I was with his size, how big he was, and how his just being hard was causing me to start dripping.

A loud groan came out of his mouth that took me off guard, and I felt my back hit the couch, I looked up at Jesse, and he was making direct eye contact with me.

I was now lying down on the couch with Jesse leaning over me.

He spread my legs even more and wrapped them around his hips.

I raised a brow, wondering what he was planning on doing, but then I felt it; he was on top of me and doing exactly what I was doing to him before, but this time, I was the one getting it done too, and I was in a laying position. The way Jesse was grinding on me caused sparks to come to my head.

I wrapped my arms around him and let him take control, liking the feeling it gave me, which drove me crazy and made my whole body feel like it was in bliss.

"Baby," I said, which had him groaning as he fastened his pace.

"You're all mine. I swear I'm all yours. You're so fucking addicting." He said; I felt my stomach tighten and knew I was going to come soon; I needed to tell him because if he didn't stop, I was definitely going to shoot my load into my underwear.

"Jesse, I'm going to come," I said, nervous about what he would do, but he didn't stop.

He quickened his pace. My eyes widened, realizing that Jesse had no interest in stopping what he was doing.

"Come, baby. I'm going to be coming right there with you," he said as soon as those words registered in my mind.

I came and Jesse came right after I did.

Saying my name as he did.

He leaned his head against my shoulder, trying to catch his breath.

I let out a chuckle and felt his lips smiling against my shoulder.

"So you're mine huh?" I asked, and he let out a chuckle.

"Every inch of me." He said softly.

(*Kassandra Speaks*)

Well, damn, that was sexy. I love them; their scenes get better and better. Give this chapter a VOTE & COMMENT

Xoxo

-Kassandra Vivu

CH. 18 I'm Smiling

C H. 18 I'm Smiling

(Ben POV)

I was working, sitting at my desk, and apparently, I was smiling.

"Well, well, well. Look who I caught with a smile on their face again." Lilian said, making her way towards me.

I let out a laugh. "Oh, wow, I also was awarded a laugh. Someone is in a good mood today. Something good must have happened," she said, pulling a seat and bringing it to my desk.

I felt my face getting heated because something good did happen.

I have a boyfriend, and he's fantastic. How should I say that? Would Lilian judge me?

If she judges me for having a boyfriend, then that would mean she's someone I don't need as a friend.

"I have a boyfriend," I said softly, watching her eyes widen and a smile pops.

"You know, I knew it had to be you meeting someone and dating now. Wow, Ben, you're off the market, huh? A lot of hearts will be broken," she said, smiling. I shook my head, chuckling at her statement.

"I don't think anyone's heart will be broken," I said, and she gave me a look while looking around.

"I'm not so sure about that, so what's your boyfriend like?" she asked, smiling at me, and I felt my face getting even hotter.

"Woah, Ben. Don't turn into a tomato in front of me. He must be pretty amazing if he has you reacting this way and all," she said.

"Who is it?" She asked me, and as much as I did like where our friendship was going, I didn't want to tell her who I was dating yet.

"Can I tell you who it is when I'm ready?" I asked her.

She looked at me with a nervous look on her face.

"Please tell me there's no one here," she said, causing me to actually let out a loud chuckle.

"No," I said between laughs.

"Thank Goodness. Well, that's fine. As long as you're happy, that's all that matters." She said, smiling at me, but her smile dropped when she looked at someone behind me.

I wondered why her smile dropped until I turned around and found Derrick staring at me.

I raised a brow at his stare and turned back to talk to Lilian.

"It's getting weird, his staring." She said, bringing herself back to staring at me.

"What do you think is his problem?" I asked her, and she shrugged.

"I don't know. At first, I thought maybe he liked you, but now I don't know." Lilian said worriedly.

"Didn't he just start this?" I asked her, and she looked at me hesitantly.

"No, he didn't just start staring at you like this. I mean, I would notice him take quick glances at you and stare a little, but the staring has changed drastically ever since you walked in on them talking about you. I'm worried," Lilian said, and seeing her facial expression confirmed she was.

"He better not be a creep or sicko, I've seen a lot of lifetime movies and I'm not trying to have my new friend be a character in a movie like that, so he needs to stay back." She said.

I nodded my head at what she said and turned back around. This time, Derrick wasn't staring at me; he was getting up to walk away.

I had never felt his staring before, but from what Lilian said, he had been staring at me for some time.

Now that I feel his stare means he has been making it obvious lately.

"Are you worried about it too?" Lilian asked me, and I turned my attention to her.

"I don't know? Should I be?" I asked her, and she took a few seconds before answering my question.

She nodded her head.

"Yes, with how people are nowadays, you should be worried," she said severely.

"Okay, what should I do?" I asked her.

"You should take notice of him if he's around you or looking at you. You also shouldn't leave work alone. I'll get off work with you and leave work with you; we'll do the buddy walk toward our cars. Also, let your boyfriend know what's going on. You might want to mention it to the boss, but tell him not to worry. Not yet; all he's done is stare. We could be overreacting, but I don't want to react to something unsettling like this. A lot of things have happened to people who don't." She said.

I nodded my head, and Lilian let out a small smile.

"You're a nice person, and you've done nothing wrong. It's good to have you as a friend, so don't worry. I got this," she said, causing me to laugh.

She laughs, letting go of my hand and running her fingers through her hair.

"You're laughing so much more, and I love it. I'm so happy. I'm literally beaming," she said, smiling, and I smiled.

"Thank you, honestly that means a lot," I said, referring to her level of care.

"It means a lot to see you, happy Ben. It really does. So where do you want to go for lunch today?" she asked me. I smiled and recommended some restaurants we could go to eat in.

While talking to her, I felt like I was being stared at, and she did, too, but neither of us looked up at who we knew was staring; we ignored it as best we could as we continued talking.

But what was Derrick's issue?

(*Kassandra Speaks*)

What do you Dolls think Derrick's issue is? Why does he keep staring at Ben like that? Did you guys like how Lilian took Ben being Gay? I did, and she's been a good friend to him. How do you Dolls think Jesse would react to the whole Derrick thing when Ben tells what else has been happening? I love the progress Ben has been making, and He's laughing more. Jesse has noticed, Lilian has seen, and Derrick has too.

Give this chapter a VOTE & COMMENT!!!!!!!!!!!!

XOXO

-Kassandra Vivu

CH. 19 I like him too

C H. 19 I like him too!

(Jesse POV)

There was a knock on the hotel door, and I already knew who it was.

I smiled as I opened the door.

"I'm here!" Amber said, throwing her hands up.

I let out a laugh and shook my head at my best friend.

"I can see that and I can hear that," I said, causing her to roll her eyes.

"So where is he? Where are you hiding him?" Amber asked.

"Who? My boyfriend isn't here yet. He'll be here soon, though," I said, watching Amber's facial reaction change.

"Oh, Boyfriend, huh? I see, I see you," she said, causing me to chuckle shyly.

"Yeah, I never thought I would ever say something like that but here we are," I said, walking towards the living room in the suite.

I sat on the couch.

Amber dropped her stuff on the floor and made her way towards me.

"Have you told the gang yet?" she asked me. The gang is what she calls my family.

"No. I actually haven't." I said; she nodded her head slowly.

"They'll be okay with it, so what's he like?" Amber asked.

For some reason, I found myself excited to describe how Ben was.

"Awww, he sounds so cute. I like it, by the way, you were describing it I can see you're falling hard for him." Amber said, I thought about what she said and nodded.

"You're right, I am," I said, her smile widening.

"Will you be able to handle it though?" She asked me.

"What do you mean?" I asked her, and she let out a sigh.

"Jesse, you're a football player. Who's dating a guy, I hate to be the one to say it but some people are jerks, some football players are jerks and they might give you a hard time." She said, and I nodded my head.

"Well, they can learn to deal with it. I know some people are going to have an issue with it, and that isn't my problem. I don't care what they think. The only person I care about and the only person's feelings I take into consideration with this whole thing is Ben," I said.

Amber clapped her hands, letting out a squeal.

"The fact that you didn't even want to do the interview," she said, causing me to roll my eyes.

"I basically hooked you both up." She said, laughing.

I shook my head at her silliness.

"Seriously though, I mean are you just interested in him or knew you were interested in men?" She asked me.

"No, I'm just interested in him, and to be quite honest, I find everything about him sexy," I said, feeling my cheeks get heated.

"Woah, woah, woah there buddy. Calm down, calm down." Amber said, fanning me with both of her hands.

I let out a laugh.

"So how are you?" I asked her, and she shrugged.

"You know just dealing with questions for you, you extended your stay and people wanted to know where you were and how you're doing. The season is going to start in a couple of months and you'll have to report back by next month so you can practice with your team." She said.

"Yeah, I'm going to tell them when I get back for practice," I said, referring to dating a man.

"Are you sure?" She asked me, and I nodded my head.

"I don't know how I'm going to tell them but I'll think about how it will be done and said. I don't want them finding out by the press, especially if Ben and I are caught by the press and exposed all over the news. You know what I mean?" I said. She smiled.

"Yeah, I respect that. Gosh, you must be really serious about this." She said, placing her hand on her chest.

"I am serious, I mean you've been with me through all my relationships and you know I haven't been serious with anyone like I'm serious with this person this soon ahead," I said.

"I can't wait to meet him! Do you think he'll like me?" she asked.

"I don't see why not, I've told him about you already and told him how you're so he doesn't get spooked or anything. So I'm sure he'll like you but of course, you would have to make a good impression on him and be respectful of the way he is. He is quite shy and I'm starting to be extremely overprotective of him." I said with a severe tone added to my voice.

"Woah, did something happen already?" She asked me.

I ran my fingers through my hair.

"Yeah, he's been having problems with these dudes at work but one of them has been creeping him out lately," I said, explaining to her the story.

"What a bunch of douchebags." She said, and I agreed.

People were real assholes.

"Does he have anyone at work?" she asked, and I nodded my head, explaining to her that his boss was quite nice to him and that he had a coworker who had become a new friend to him.

"That's nice of her, honestly. He sounds like someone I will adore and maybe I might even act a little overprotective over him too. Who knows." She said, making my heart leap to see how accepting my best friend was with all of this.

She is honestly a good person.

"You know you're a great best friend right?" I asked her, and she nodded her head, laughing.

"Yes, I know." She said.

A knock came from the door, and I got up and walked towards it.

I opened the door and saw Ben.

I smiled at him.

"Hey there, handsome," I said, getting a smile from him.

I moved aside so he could come in.

I closed the door and decided to introduce him to Amber.

"Ben, this is my crazy best friend Amber, who's also my agent, which I've told you about. Amber, this is Ben, my boyfriend." I said, watching Ben's eyes widen, but smiled towards Amber anyway.

He has to get used to being called boyfriend because that was what he was.

My boyfriend.

"Nice to meet you," Amber said, giving him a hug. I was surprised that Ben hugged her back, smiling.

"Nice to meet you, too. I've heard a lot about you," he said.

"Good things, I know." She said, causing Ben to chuckle.

"You two sit, go sit. I'll go get us some snacks." I said, leaving my best friend and boyfriend together.

I smiled as I watched Amber talk to Ben. Ben was smiling, and all nervousness had left his body; I could tell he was starting to relax, which made me happy.

I felt proud.

I am proud of my best friend for being the sweetest person ever and even more proud of my boyfriend, who I can see slowly coming out of his shell.

(*Kassandra Speaks*)

Of course, when you start dating someone and build their confidence, you see that they begin to bloom and grow into the beautiful person that you know they are. I'm positive that is how Jesse feels about Ben. I love how excellent Amber is about Jesse and Ben dating. She's so supportive.

Give this chapter a VOTE & COMMENT!!!!!

Xoxo

-Kassandra Vivu

CH. 20 Acceptance is Nice

C H. 20 Acceptance is nice

(Ben POV)

Amber and I were talking. Initially nervous, but her personality and how she spoke to me put me at ease.

She was one of those people whose voice and personality made you feel comfortable; how she stared at you as she spoke made you feel like you mattered.

I felt all nervousness leave my body as she continued to tell me childhood stories about Jesse, which made me laugh quite a bit.

"Yeah, so he's a knucklehead. I am glad you're handling that well," she said, smiling.

"Yeah, he's a good guy," I said; she raised a brow.

"Yes he is, so tell me about yourself. Only if you're comfortable about telling me things, you don't have to. I just want to get to know you better that's all, you're dating my best friend after all." She said, and I nodded my head.

That was understandable.

"Sure, Uh. I'll try to answer your questions, but if I can't, I'll tell you." I said, and she nodded her head.

"Okay, that's okay. Let's see. Do you like your job?" she asked me.

"Yes, I started off as an intern but immediately got hired after my internship while others didn't. I guess the boss saw potential in me," I said.

"That's a good thing, Ben. That means you're really good. It takes a lot for someone to take you in and let you part of their business, especially when they saw the potential in you through your internship." She said, smiling.

I felt my face getting hot. I was still getting used to being praised in specific ways.

"Awe, you're cute. Okay, next question. Do you have any friends at work or outside of work?" She asked me if I thought of Lilian and mentioned her to Amber.

Amber asked me a couple of more questions, not too serious ones that would have me feeling uncomfortable.

I didn't like talking about my childhood. It wasn't the best, and I wanted to avoid discussing it.

Discussing it would instantly shift the mood, and I didn't want that.

Amber seems really cool, and I liked her. I didn't want either of us to feel uncomfortable.

"Hey, you two, getting to know each other?" Jesse came to the living room with a tray filled with snacks.

"Yes, honestly, Ben is a sweetheart. You're a lucky dude. Now, bring the snacks here. I'm trying to snack myself away," Amber said, getting a laugh from Jesse.

He passed her the snack tray.

Sitting next to me, pulling me into his arms.

"So what do you guys want to do?" Jesse asked, kissing my head.

Amber shrugged her shoulder; it surprised me how she took this so casually.

I mean, most people would look at us in shock, especially if they knew someone like Jesse, who they thought was a heterosexual, suddenly was dating this man.

But Amber acted like it was nothing and kept eating the snacks.

"I wanted to go view the city, you know, take it all in since I'm on break. I don't know, maybe meet someone or something," she said.

"You can come to hang out with me and my friend Lilian tomorrow; she's doing something in the city," I said; her eyes widened.

"Sure if you don't mind," she said, I shook my head, saying it was fine.

"Um, am I invited too?" Jesse asked.

I giggled, "Of course." We sat there, talking about anything, really, and I quite enjoyed it.

I liked Amber's personality, and I could already tell that I would get along with her.

It surprised me how someone could just come into my life and have me actually open myself to opportunities that I would have never found myself doing or even thinking about.

There was no way I would quickly have spoken to someone as I did with Amber today.

I didn't like putting myself out there, and it didn't matter if it was just regarding friendship, either.

That's just how I was.

Amber, later on, left and went to her own hotel room.

It was me and Jesse now.

"So, how was your day?" He asked me, pulling myself closer to him.

I told him about my day, including the staring I got today.

He looked at me concerned.

"Okay, I'm getting worried now. What's his problem, there has to be something going on with that dude." Jesse said, and I sighed.

I cuddled closer into his arms, loving how his scent filled my nose.

He always smelled so amazing.

"I know but he hasn't done anything to me, so that's saying something," I said, Jesse suddenly tightened his arms around me.

"We're not waiting for him to do something, no. Please promise me that you will talk to your boss about this the next time you go to work. This is serious Ben, we don't know what's in his thoughts or heart. You don't know what he's capable of." He said, and I nodded my head, understanding what he meant.

He was right; the staring could mean many things, and I would take this seriously.

"Okay, I'll talk to my boss the next time I go to work. I promise." I said.

He turned us around so he was on top of me.

He looked down at me and smiled.

"That's Good, so I'm going to tell my Mother about you tomorrow," he said, taking me off guard.

I stared at him, stunned.

"Are you sure you're ready to?" I asked him, concerned that he might regret something later.

"Yes, of course. I'm serious about you after all. So yes, I am ready to tell my mom that I got into a serious relationship with someone who I happen to be very serious about." He said, causing me to roll my eyes and chuckle.

"Okay, Jesse. Okay." I said; a smirk appeared on his face, and he pressed his lips against mine.

The warmth I felt when Jesse kissed me was something I wanted to experience for a very long time.

After he was done kissing me, he looked down at me with a gentle look.

"Can.... can we learn more about each other?" I asked him, his eyes widened.

"I want us to just learn more about each other regarding anything and everything," I said.

"Of course Baby, you can tell me anything. I'll be here, I promise." He said.

Jesse's words made me want to open up to him about certain things that I didn't think I would open up to anyone about.

"Okay... well, here's the story." I started to say to him.

CH. 21 My story to you

C H. 21 My Story to You

(Ben POV)

I was nervous about telling him the story, telling him my story.

I looked at him, and he had a gentle expression on his face, which brought me calmness.

I found myself calm around Jesse; it was new and something I had never thought I would experience. That was honesty right there.

I couldn't believe someone could help me feel this way, with them just being around me or caring for me.

"I was in the foster care system all my life, the foster care system wasn't the best. As a matter of fact, some of them were extremely awful. I got physically abused and even almost got sexually abused in some too, I always ended up always getting out of those ones somehow and being placed in another foster home right after." I said, staring at my hand.

"I had to be on the lookout for not only bad foster parents but also twisted and bad foster siblings. I kept to myself and I guess some people felt like they could easily mess with someone like that." I said, flinching as I recalled some memories.

I kept talking, not wanting to look up at Jesse yet.

"I was an easy target to bullies at school and in the system, even the adults were bullies. It was when I was 15 years old that I was actually brought to a good foster care home. The woman was very nice and I was her only foster care child. She gave me my own room, my first birthday and made me feel safe. It took me a while to feel comfortable, I kept thinking it was a dream, that she wasn't going to want me around. She was amazing." I said, remembering her; she was the most beautiful woman I've ever seen. Some looks were given to us, what would a grown black woman want with a white foster kid.

"She tried hiding it from me that she was sick. She did a good job at it in the beginning, but I wasn't a dumb kid, and she always pointed out that to me. I continued working hard in school, got many scholarships and she was proud of me. It was when she fell to the floor that my suspicions were right. When we got to the hospital, it was confirmed that she had cancer. She knew, but she kept it from me, claiming she didn't want to trouble me." I said, feeling tears fall down my eyes.

"Imagine that. I finally found a good human being in my life, a woman who made me feel loved and wanted. A woman who gave me a mother's love, and now she was being ripped away from me," I said, shaking my head.

"I hated it. I wanted all her pain to go to the people who hurt me instead. As a matter of fact, I prayed for that. The fact that had me going crazy more was that she continued acting normal for me. I knew she was in pain, but she continued asking me about the school, paying for classes that I wanted to take as extras, and helping me with my essays for scholarships and my reports." I said, smiling at the thoughts.

"The doctors tried with chemo, they really did but it didn't work. She kept telling me that if she had met me sooner, that she would have been more strong enough to fight. That she's been in the foster system herself and outgrew foster case. That she also never got adopted, but she worked for everything she had. She was also helping someone else in a similar situation like me as well, and she wanted us to meet. She was strong though, the day that I'll never forget with her. Is when she handed me papers, she had a smile on her face when she did." I said, remembering the moment.

"They were adoption papers?" Jesse asked softly.

I nodded my head.

"Of course I was happy, I even asked her if I could call her Mom and I remember the joy that filled her face. I finally had a mom. We worked hard and got my last name changed to hers. I became Ben Robinson." I said, smiling.

My smile fell.

"Of course life just had to ruin it somehow, she died a couple of months after my 18th-year-old birthday, but she left me so much things and what was extremely crazy is that she had a storage room filled with things that she bought me, things she thought I would enjoy, she had an apartment ready for me and everything, she did that for me and the other girl she wanted to adopt." I said, shaking my head.

"That woman," I said, finding myself crying.

"I wish I met her sooner, I wish her and I met sooner. I was so angry with everything, I was angry with life. I finally had a good thing happen to me and I lost her. I was there on her last day. We spoke and laughed about things, she was strong for me. That was the first time anyone has ever told me they loved me. That was the first time I've ever told anyone I loved them.

I told her that she was my mother, the best mother I could ever ask for and love. I was happy to get the chance to be her son." I said, letting out a laugh.

"It was so mess up, I was finally someone's son and It wasn't even for that long, I was going to be someones brother and I was going to have a family." I said, shaking my head.

"She smiled at me, told me from the minute I entered her home, I became her son that day," I said, remembering how my heart felt when she said that.

"I laid my head on her lap as she played with my hair. I was there with her until the moment she left me. Never left her side." I said, looking up at Jesse.

Tears were in her eyes.

"What was her name?" He asked me.

I smiled.

"Analiese Robinson, that was my mom's name," I said.

Jesse moved up to me and pulled me into his arms.

"God Baby, I'm so sorry." He said.

I wrapped my arms around Jesse as well. Letting myself get comfortable in his arms.

"I just get scared sometimes, that every good thing that happens to me won't last." I found myself saying.

I was being honest with him, being honest with my feelings.

I felt his arms around me tighten.

"That won't happen," he said, and even with him saying that, I couldn't believe it.

I so badly wanted to, but it's just something that I've always had happened to me.

He pulled himself back and looked at me.

"I'll make sure of it." He said, looking at me with a serious expression.

"You deserve happiness and I'll make sure of it." He said.

CH: 22 I'm staying

- -

C H: 22 I'm staying

(Jesse POV)

I know it took a lot for Ben to open up to me like he did, and I couldn't blame him.

I sat up with him, pulling him into a hug. "Thank you for telling me this, I know it took a lot for you to," I said, kissing his forehead.

"Did you ever find out about the other girl? The one she was looking into adopting as well?" I asked him. Ben shook his head, saying no.

I could look into it for him if he wanted to contact her; I held that thought in my head and made a note to bring it up later.

For now, I just held Ben in my arms and rubbed his back, hoping it would soothe him, I didn't know what kind of past Ben had, but I can say that I didn't think it would be this bad.

I can't imagine the abuse he's gone through, and just the thought of it made me feel horrible.

Nothing like this is ever going to happen to him again.

I ran my fingers through Ben's hair and cuddled him even closer.

When did I become this sweet? I found myself wanting to do so many lovely things to this man.

I wanted to make him feel like he was always on cloud nine.

"Do you want something to eat, baby?" I said, kissing his forehead.

"I can make you something, or we can order takeout," I said.

Ben sniffed and lifted his head; my heart tightened as soon as I saw his face.

"Gosh, baby," I said, kissing his lips.

"I'm sorry you didn't have to tell me, I hope I didn't force you to," I said, feeling guilty. Ben shook his head.

"No I wanted to, and I'm okay with takeout." He said, smiling sadly.

"I meant what I said, Ben, I am serious about us and want to be in your life long-term. I promise." I said to him, rubbing my hand on his cheek.

"I might get annoying though," I said, causing him to laugh.

"I don't think I'll find you annoying." He said.

"Are you sure? I mean, I'm going to want your attention every day. I want to talk to you every day and hear from you. I'm going to want to be around you a lot." I said softly; this was something I was a little insecure about. I didn't want to be overbearing or someone that got annoying. Especially knowing that I really like Ben and want to do all these things with him.

"Yes, I am sure. I would like all of that and would have no issue with any of it," he said, staring at me.

"Good. So what would my baby like to eat?" I asked, kissing his cheek.

"We can order anything you want," I said, kissing his lips.

"We can order Chinese." He said, kissing me back.

"Yeah, we can do that. Let's see if we can find a good place nearby." I said, taking out my phone.

"Do you want to borrow some of my comfortable clothes?" I asked him, and a blush appeared on Ben's face.

"If you don't mind." He said.

I held back a laugh.

"Yes, we both should change and I don't mind at all. I'm actually looking forward to seeing you in my clothes." I said, standing up with him in my arms.

I watched Ben's eyes widen as I carried him into the bedroom.

"Bet you didn't think I would be able to carry you huh?" I asked him.

"No, I actually didn't." He said, causing me to laugh.

"Do you mind it?" I asked him.

"No, not at all." He said.

I gently let him down inside the bedroom and entered the closet to find something to wear. I handed him a T-shirt and sweatpants.

"Is this okay?" I asked Ben.

"Yes, it's fine. Thank you." He said, taking the clothes from me.

"You can change in the attached bathroom," I said, pointing to where it was.

"Okay." He said, walking away. I watched Ben go into the bathroom and close the door behind him.

Fuck.

I wore those clothes yesterday night and slept in them. They didn't smell badly, but I knew they smelled like me, and I wanted to see him in them badly.

I wanted to see him wearing something that's mine. Something that had my scent on it.

I leaned against the wall, clearing my thoughts. I needed to calm down, now wasn't the time to be horny over my boyfriend.

I returned to the closet, taking out clothes to wear. I removed my clothes and put them in the laundry basket.

I was wearing sweatpants when Ben came out; I immediately focused on him when he did.

I stood there still, staring at him. Something about him wearing my clothes was driving me crazy.

"You look good," I said, finding my voice hoarse.

"Thank you," Ben said shyly.

His eyes fluttered to my chest, and I remembered I didn't have a shirt.

I chuckled.

"Like what you see?" I asked him as I grabbed a shirt.

"Yes," Ben said, causing me to stop.

"Do you?" I asked him as I made my way towards him.

"Because I like what I see too," I said, leaning him against the wall.

"Very much," I said, pulling him into a kiss. Ben kissed me back with no hesitation; I groaned as I let my hand roam down his body. I didn't miss the fact that he was hard again.

I pulled my lips back and looked at him. He was staring at me as well; there was so much passion in his eyes that I felt like I was being devoured right there.

"The way you're staring at me right now is driving me crazy," I said, clearing my throat.

"Is it bothering you?" He asked softly.

"No, of course not. It's tempting me, though." I said, clearing my throat again. I took a few steps back.

"Tempting you to do what?" he asked me. I stared at him for a minute, noticing how he looked.

He was wearing my clothes; he was naked underneath my clothes right now.

"Ben," I said.

"Jesse." He said, causing me to moan from him just saying my name.

"You haven't been with anyone else before have you?" I asked him, knowing the answer already.

"No." He said.

I lowered my gaze and brought my attention back to his face. Ben was still staring at me.

"I should calm down," I said, chuckling.

"Why?" Ben asked, tilting his head.

"Because I want to touch you." I found myself saying.

"Then touch me," Ben said softly.

A thrill ran through my body; I shook my head and lowered my gaze to the sweatpants. I could see that Ben was hard. I wanted to do something I had never done before, which excited me and made me nervous.

"I don't just want to touch you, though," I said, bringing my attention back to his face.

"Then what else?" He asked.

"I want to taste you," I said, not letting my eyes waver from his. Ben's eyes widened as the words registered to him.

"What do you want to taste?" He whispered.

I moved closer to him and let my eyes trail down his body to where his cock was.

"Your cock." I said, staring at his hard-on.

"You said I could touch you," I said, rubbing my hand against his hard-on. A moan came from Ben; I returned my stare to his face and found his eyes fluttered close.

"Jesse." He said.

"You said I could touch you," I said, putting my hand inside the sweatpants. I wrapped my hand around his cock, moaning at the fact that he was completely naked underneath the sweatpants.

Ben moaned as I rubbed the tip of his cock.

"Yes, I did." He said, opening his eyes.

"But can I taste you?" I asked him, staring at him.

"Yes." He said softly.

"Mmm," I said, lowering myself; I removed my hand away from Ben's cock.

He let out a groan, but his breath hitched when I lowered his pants.

I stared at his cock; it was big.

For the first time, I can admit that I found someone's cock pretty.

This will be my first time doing this, and I am still determining whether I will be good at it.

Yet, I found myself wanting to take Ben into my mouth.

"Fuck." I said as I brought my tongue out and licked Ben's cock. A loud moan came from him, and his fingers were immediately on my hair.

I licked him again, this time taking him into my mouth and started to suck him off, there was a precum on his tip, and I found myself rolling my tongue on the tip of his cock, which caused Ben to moan even more. I continued sucking, licking, and twirling my tongue around him; the room was filled with his moans.

Ben was moaning my name and tugging on my hair, which was turning me on even more.

I looked up to find Ben staring at me; for some reason, I became harder just from that interaction. Him staring at me as I suck him off was getting me hot. I pulled him out of my mouth and licked him.

"Jesse," Ben said, moaning my name.

"Yes, baby?" I asked, not breaking eye contact with him.

I brought my tongue to the tip of his cock and licked it.

Ben moaned and tightened the grip on my hair.

"Do you like that?" I asked him.

"Yes." He said, groaning.

I took him into my mouth again, and he moaned; his breathing was picking up.

"Jesse. I'm going to cum." He said; he tried pulling my head back, but I didn't move.

"Jesse. I'm going to cum." He said, but I sucked him faster.

"Baby." He moaned and cummed in my mouth. My eyes widened, being slightly taken off guard on how much was in my mouth and the taste of it.

"Oh my gosh, spit it out." He said as I took him out of my mouth. I stood up and swallowed it.

His eyes widened even more as he stared at me.

"Spitting is for quitters," I said, shrugging.

All of this was new to me, I had just sucked a dick for the first time and swallowed come, so I looked away shyly, not knowing what to say after that.

"Did you like it?" I asked him nervously.

"Like it?" he asked breathlessly. I turned my attention to him and found him staring at me, his eyes lowering down my body.

I lowered my gaze, knowing I was also hard.

Ben lowered himself in front of me.

"Ben you don't have to." I said to him.

He looked up at me.

"You don't want me to?" He asked.

"No, it's not that. It's just you don't have to." I said, groaning when he pulled my cock out.

"I want to." He said, taking me into his mouth.

"Fuck, baby," I said as he moved his head up and down while he sucked me off.

My eyes widened; the way Ben was sucking my cock was driving me crazy.

"Ben," I said as I felt him rub his tongue on the vein underneath my cock.

My eyes widened.

Ben was good at this.

"Fuck, Ben. Why are you good at this?" I asked him, and he hummed around my cock, which caused me to throw my head back and moan. He pulled back and twirled his tongue up and down my cock; I stared down at Ben, sucking me off, and he was making direct eye contact with me as he did so.

"Fuck, you're so sexy," I said, tugging his hair. A smile came to his face as he took me out of his mouth.

Shit. I said, watching him smile as he licked me. He brought his tongue to my balls, and I held my breath as he took one of them into his mouth.

My grip tightened on his hair.

"Ben," I said as I shivered.

He took my cock into his mouth again and quickened his pace.

"Ben," I said, losing control and letting myself fall into complete bliss.

"Baby. I'm going to cum." I said, removing my hands from his hair so he could pull back.

Ben surprised me by putting my hands on his head again.

"Baby. I'm going to cum you should move." I said, knowing that I was going to cum soon, but Ben kept sucking on my cock even more.

"Fuck." I said cumming.

Some of my cum came out of Ben's mouth, I heard a gulp which shocked me, and Ben continued licking my cock, taking the drips of cum with his tongue.

I stood there breathless, hot, horny, and wondering how the hell he was so good at this.

He stood up, looking at me, laughing nervously.

"I'm gay, I've done research and watched videos on how to please my future partner." He said shyly.

"Were you pleased?" He asked me.

"Yes," I said in a whisper.

I have never found myself feeling this way before.

"I'm glad, baby," Ben said, kissing my cheek.

My eyes fluttered close.

Ben had me feeling so many new things right now, and I hope I was doing the same for him.